T0194340

LOSS

Also by William M. Gould

Partners
A Little Score to Settle
Three Boys Like You
The Note Played Next

LOSS

AND OTHER STORIES

WILLIAM M. GOULD

iUniverse

LOSS
AND OTHER STORIES

iUniverse books may be ordered through booksellers or by contacting:

iUniverse
1663 Liberty Drive
Bloomington, IN 47403
www.iuniverse.com
1-800-Authors (1-800-288-4677)

ISBN: 978-1-4917-8867-7 (sc)
ISBN: 978-1-4917-8866-0 (e)

Library of Congress Control Number: 2016902120

Print information available on the last page.

iUniverse rev. date: 02/17/2016

Always, for Sue

STORIES

THE TRAIN FROM VICTORIA FALLS

THE BOY WAS DEAD—CRUSHED by the wheels of the train. A murmur spread through the car and Peter heard someone say, "Oh, Jesus—oh, my God," softly, as if praying for everyone. Like candles flickering out, the alcoholic glow of the students and the rugby players vanished, and in its place fearful sobriety appeared in blanched faces. The girl who had thrown the money down on the platform screamed once and began sobbing. Mrs. Storck became very agitated and twisted her damp handkerchief around her fingers.

Below, along the side of the train, there was an awful wailing and the shouting of excited voices. They were carrying away the body and one of the conductors was talking to a group of men who were probably the important people in the village.

Baker, the elderly doctor from Capetown, had grasped the handrail and was trying to climb back on the train, but a woman held him back. Tears streamed down her black face and she was saying something to him that he seemed to understand. He reached out and held her gently by the shoulder. With his little white beard and spectacles he seemed a kindly saint giving sad comfort to her, and then she turned away and walked toward the others. The train began to move again as Dr. Baker climbed up the steps.

Peter sat down in his seat at the end of the railway car. In the chill of late afternoon the African sun focused a bit of warmth through the glass window and it felt good against his shoulder. He took up the unfinished letter to his parents that lay on the cushion where he'd left it, and with his pen began to trace the last words he had written.

I met them at Victoria Falls—two South African
couples (about your age)—and we have spent the last

1

> *few days together. You would probably get along with*
> *them—they like the good life.*

"We don't see many Americans here," Mrs. Storck had said that first July day. Peter and the two South African couples were sitting at a white painted wrought-iron table under an enormous spreading tree on the grounds of the hotel.

"Rhodesia's a bit off the path for you, isn't it?" Mrs. Storck went on. It was 1974.

Peter told them about the Peace Corps. "I'm stationed next door in Botswana," he said. "I took two weeks of leave to drift around."

"Drifting?" asked Mrs. Storck disapprovingly from under her large sun hat.

Yes, Peter thought. Drifting. That's what his father had called the whole adventure. And it was, of course—a letting go. He had cut himself loose from his parents in that moment when he had mailed the application to Washington and had suddenly felt as if anything might happen.

"And have you made the most of your holiday?" asked Mrs. Baker. Peter regarded her across the table. She is like Mother, he realized— life as a serious business.

"I'm having lots of adventures," he said. "Meeting people, seeing things." He suspected it might have sounded peculiar, or even juvenile, but they all nodded and let it pass. It was so pleasant and easy sitting there under the tree and it seemed as though blocks of time might be slipping by. He savored the luxury of feeling the afternoon move in upon them.

It's like summer on Long Island, he thought. The deep green shade with the sunny lawn beyond. The ice clinking in the glasses. The well-dressed foursome sitting around the table with him. Only this was Rhodesia. Forget about Long Island. This was real.

What a lovely day! He wanted always to remember it and forced himself to an exquisite awareness of detail—Mr. Storck's pastel tie, the sounds of children splashing in the hotel's swimming pool, an ant moving a breadcrumb on the patio. He felt free, with no responsibility except to himself. He could call this his own experience. It wasn't his father's. It wasn't from a book.

Earlier that morning Peter had walked down to the falls. He stood in the lush rain forest that grows on the edges of the gorge, clouds of spray wrapping him in fine mist. The great Zambezi dropped over the steep ledge in a stupendous thundering flow. Time after time he had succumbed to the temptation of allowing his eye to abandon itself in the foaming green water at the brink, and then to follow its inevitable plunging line of fall down past jutting rocks and tenacious trees until it was lost in the billowing spume below. When he looked up he'd found himself dizzy and it seemed that everything was falling, even the very ledge over which the falls poured.

It was there in the rain forest that he had met the Bakers. He'd noticed them in the dining room at breakfast and then again as they stood quite near looking out over the splendid scene. They'd fallen into conversation and afterwards the three had walked down the path together. He had liked them at once. Mrs. Baker seemed to Peter a propelling force. Her vivacity and energy drove them along, stopping now and then to comment eagerly on a new bird or flower spied in the undergrowth. She was a large freckled woman with a maternal vitality that Peter felt right away. And yet how different from Mother, he thought. Not at all nervous, but no *chic* either. She wore a plain print dress and sturdy walking shoes. The Bakers were on a short holiday traveling about in Rhodesia.

"We're South African," the doctor had said, holding aside a large dripping branch for his wife. "We can't go to very many places." His pale blue eyes appraised Peter.

"Rhodesia, of course," he continued. "And naturally we pass through Botswana en route between the two countries. But, that's all."

Not hard to understand why, Peter knew. He felt he was expected to say something. "Maybe things will get better," he said.

"The black countries don't want us," the doctor said. "We can't even get a visa. A shame. I was in Tanganyika before the war. Wonderful game. But we can't go there now."

"Yes," said Peter. "Too bad."

A lifetime under the African sun had dappled the doctor's Celtic face with brown macules and little crusted flakes. There was an air of gentle dignity about him. He wore tweeds that were too large for his frail structure. They had strolled along together, stopping at each new view of the falls, chatting, telling one another about their travels.

3

"Look there at the island just above the brink," said Dr. Baker, pointing across the gorge. "That's where David Livingstone landed in his canoe when he saw the falls for the first time." The doctor was a great admirer of Livingstone.

"You'd be interested to see his old house," said Peter. "It's near my village. He built it himself and his kids were born there. It's just a pile of stones in the desert now."

They had walked up the path and across the wide lawn to the hotel reposing in its aura of colonial splendor.

"Grass! Lovely, cool grass," said Peter, bending down to brush the soft green turf with his palm. "It's like home."

"But not Botswana, eh?" said Mrs. Baker. They all laughed.

"What is your village like?" asked the doctor.

For an instant Peter saw his village—the glare and dust; the eager black faces in the crowded schoolroom where he taught English.

"Flat and dusty," he said. "And they're wonderful people—kind and generous. I won't mind going back."

Oh, no, he thought. Why did I put it that way? Not *mind* going back? I'm betraying them. Just talking about them to these people is betrayal. He picked up his binoculars and searched the branches overhead. There were birds everywhere and for a few moments he lost himself in nature. The Bakers said nothing, and it took only a few moments for Peter to put the uncomfortable thought out of his mind.

The other couple, the Storcks, came by and they all moved to the broad veranda of the hotel where they sipped iced lemonade and cold beer. Mrs. Storck looked pale and tired, and in her dark glasses and floppy brimmed hat reminded Peter of a languid and deadly toadstool. He thought Mrs. Baker was just barely suppressing a look of annoyance. Storck was a plethoric, heavily built man with a gruff voice. He appeared affable at first, but became wary after Peter mentioned the Peace Corps.

"Botswana, eh?" said Storck, his eyebrows going up. "I daresay they can use a bright young man like you. But, come on—teaching? It would do them more good if you taught them the value of hard work."

Peter began to say something, but Storck interrupted him. "You ought to come down and see South Africa, too. It's a beautiful, beautiful country and you'd miss so much if you don't spend a few weeks."

Peter hesitated an instant. Storck looked like his father.

"Yes, I'd like that. I suppose I should, shouldn't I?" he said. Something made him think that Storck was going to continue, perhaps to tell a racial joke the way his father might. But, Storck merely poured some more beer for himself.

Out beyond the beds of red and yellow flowers at the end of the lawn, the white vapor from the falls hung over the gorge in a great cloud. Peter could see the inert line of freight cars that blocked the steel arch railway bridge connecting Zambia with Rhodesia.

"Such a lovely view," said Mrs. Baker dreamily.

"How long have those railroad cars been there?" Peter asked.

The doctor laughed.

"You see," he said. "The border is officially closed. Hostile governments, you know. But, business goes on. Zambian copper moves south during the night when it doesn't embarrass anyone."

Mrs. Storck perked up. Her daughter was married to an Army man and she'd heard about the importance of copper.

"The Communists would love to get that copper," she said knowingly.

"What Communists?" Peter asked.

"Why the Russians, of course. Or the Chinese. They'd be here in a minute if it weren't for us."

"Oh, come on," said Peter. "That sounds like an excuse."

"You Americans are too idealistic," said Storck, leaning forward in his chair. "You should come to South Africa. Then you'd know what problems we have. People are very quick to criticize, but they don't really know what it's like," he rasped.

Mrs. Baker blushed and turned nervously in her chair.

"You people have some pretty bad race problems, too," said Storck, persisting and waving a sausage-like index finger at Peter. "You haven't been able to solve them either."

Mrs. Storck looked quite pleased with this. She gave a thin little smile in Peter's direction and made small nodding motions of approval. Dr. Baker gave a little cough and Peter understood it to be a sign not to pay too much attention to Storck. The Bakers clearly had little use for the Storcks and this eased the awkwardness of the situation for Peter.

"Where do you live in America?" asked Mrs. Baker.

"In a little town outside of New York City," Peter said.

How odd . . . mentioning New York while sitting there under the spreading tree, conscious of Africa and the waiters who moved back and forth across the lawn. He began to tell them about the United States, nothing unusual, just the ordinary things that everyone knew about anyway. Nothing about his father who was a self-made man and who would have mentioned selling newspapers as a youth on the freezing streets of Manhattan. Nothing about his mother whose life was filled with golf and clothes and who had said more than once that none of the children could ever be the man their father was.

Across the veranda a marimba band made up of young African boys began to play. Barefoot and in white shorts, they stood laughing behind the instruments, hammering out light wooden resonances and broken rhythms into a melody full of nostalgia.

After a while Peter stood up.

"I'll see you all later, at dinner perhaps," he said.

The bell captain stood behind the counter and surveyed the lobby. Two black porters waited quietly nearby. One leaned against the desk and the other stood slightly out on the floor and looked up at the big clock. The bell captain had the military bearing and open faced friendliness of an ex-non-commissioned officer in Her Majesty's forces, a man one might count on to solve a problem or help one out of a difficulty.

Peter walked over and asked about making a long distance telephone call to Botswana. "I want to call a friend to tell him to pick me up when the train gets in."

The bell captain leaned forward across the desk resting on his forearms. "Gaborone? We can put it through, Sir," he said. "I'll have you paged when it comes in, or you can take it in your room, Sir." He stood up and pulled at a corner of his moustache.

"I'll just wait here. How long will it be?"

"Oh, it will surely take two hours, Sir."

"Two hours!" Peter was astounded. "Why so long?"

"Oh, Sir, you must know. The Africans. They run the whole show down there in Botswana, even the phones. They can never do anything right."

"That's a helluva thing to say," said Peter. The bell captain straightened his shoulders and blinked.

Storck and his wife had come along to get the key to their room. Peter shot a glance at them and detected a glimmer of smile in Storck's beefy face. Had they heard? Or was it a reflection of his own embarrassment? He saw that the black porters had moved away.

"I'll take the call in my room," said Peter.

"Very well, Sir."

That night they all ate together in the spacious dining salon. It was a quiet and subdued room done in tones of green and gray. The floor was carpeted and a large cut-glass chandelier hung from the high ceiling. Formally attired black waiters bearing large trays and silver pitchers moved about silently among the tables. Small explosions of laughter and chatter in French and German could be made out in the general humming and droning of conversation.

Peter had felt uneasy being so much younger than the others, but they seemed particularly to enjoy his inexperience. Mrs. Baker adopted the role of mother and took great interest in the practical details of Peter's travels about Africa, notably things having to do with meals and ways of avoiding dysentery. This was one of the few times in over a year when Peter had sat down at a table like this, wearing a tie and jacket, and dining with people who looked like his parents. His mind wandered and he was surprised to find himself thinking of a Setswana proverb he'd heard in his village.

When the leopard pounces, men have no tribe.

This image of sudden violence in the desert took hold of his mind for a moment. He looked beyond the table and as he scanned the faces of other diners in the elegant room he knew he was changed. He would never be the same boy who had arrived in the village, tired and scared, a year ago.

Storck was enjoying the meal. He attacked a roasted guinea fowl enthusiastically and urged the others to taste samples of it.

"Wonderful," he beamed at the company, wiping his lips. He finished the wine in his glass.

"What's this? We've run out of wine," he said. "Here, you! Boy!" he waved to a waiter. "Get us another bottle of this wine."

Peter looked at Mrs. Baker who was staring fixedly at her plate.

"Doesn't it seem awkward to you?" Peter asked, looking at all of them. "The blacks doing all the work, the whites giving the orders?"

Storck sat up straight and pushed his chair back. "Just a minute, Peter," he said. "It's a simple question of numbers. We're in the minority and we have to be strong to keep our rights. Tell him, Doctor. It's true, eh?"

Mrs. Storck nodded approvingly.

The doctor raised his eyebrows and appeared thoughtful for a moment.

"It's very difficult," he sighed. "You're right, but things are evolving. We are going to have to accept some inevitable changes."

Peter avoided the South Africans the next day. They were all taking the evening train that began at Victoria Falls and traveled south through Botswana into South Africa. He was irritated by Storck and disliked the feeling they all gave him of confinement and restriction. The Bakers were fine, he thought, but they will be with Storck and his wife. Better to go off alone. He went into town looking in the stores and curio shops, and then walked along the rain forest path again. After lunch he read in the garden and began a long letter to his parents. As he read it over he was quite pleased with its exotic description of the falls.

At five o'clock he went back to his room. Anticipating the two-day train trip and its inconveniences, he moved slowly as he collected his things and laid fresh clothing on the bed. He undressed and went into the bathroom to shave. It the mirror he looked past his lather-covered face and saw the handle of the bedroom door turn. He reached for a towel just as the maid walked in. She stood in the doorway with eyes averted, a young black girl trying to be invisible.

"Like the bed turned down, Sir?" she asked, pretending not to see him.

"No, no. I'm taking the train now," he said quickly. She smiled and closed the door.

Peter completed his preparations hurriedly and got dressed. Picking up his bag, he left the room and carried it down the long cream-colored hall to the lobby. A few tourists were browsing at the newsstand. He stepped outside into the garden at the front of the hotel. In the mild early evening golden dust motes hung suspended and settled slowly into the grass. The opulent flowers touched by the waning light seemed even more lush and vivid than at midday. He began the short walk to the rail station along a road shaded by tall trees with great overhanging branches.

The thought of the journey by train for this part of his trip made him happy. It seemed an escape into an earlier period when things moved more slowly and with more grace. There was the station building ahead with its gabled roof and gingerbread woodwork, another relic of the past. He remembered back to the day when he had left for Africa. His father, silent and fearful, driving the Chrysler along the Belt Parkway; his mother, looking pale and dabbing at her eyes with a tissue.

"I can't believe you're going," she had said. "Africa! Why?"

"Enough," said his father quietly, waving his hand at her. When they got to the terminal Peter saw the other volunteers standing in a group and he insisted his parents drop him off. He couldn't have them waiting there with him. Afterwards he stood on the curb, blinking as the car pulled out into the stream of traffic, his mother turning in the seat and clutching her wet tissue.

The brown cars painted with yellow letters saying "Rhodesia Railways" waited along the track belching puffs of steam. He saw the Bakers getting aboard up ahead, the doctor, thin, almost fragile, waiting below as Mrs. Baker in her flowered dress was given a hand up by the conductor. On the platform a large party of students milled about laughing and joking. A South African rugby team was leaving after a victorious match and the train was filling up with players, girlfriends and students. Whiffs of beer and hints of perfume wafted over Peter as he waded through the boisterous crowd.

The train hurtled along through the night past unseen villages. Peter slept fitfully in the narrow berth, waking now and then to peer through the window at the dark featureless earth. He could hear unsteady voices and merriment growing louder as some students lurched along the passageway. They stopped outside his compartment and banged on the door.

"Hey, Yank. Wake up! Have a beer, mate," said one. Peter pulled the blanket over his head. The students moved on singing a blurred chorus. He fell asleep and dreamt of water cascading down the gorge and of sipping beer on the hotel lawn.

In the morning the sun streamed into his compartment and Peter looked out as the train moved steadily across the flat red earth. At some point during early afternoon they passed into Botswana. Alone in his compartment, he stretched out his legs and put down the newspaper he'd finished reading. He watched some brightly colored birds perching on the wires that ran along the track, but his eyes soon tired of it and, yawning, his gaze shifted back into the compartment. He heard people coming along the passageway. It was the doctor and his wife. There was a knock.

"We're going up for tea," said Mrs. Baker. "Come join us."

Peter opened the door.

"Thank you," he said. "That sounds good."

Mrs. Baker led the way. The train bounced and vibrated rhythmically as they maneuvered down the aisle.

"Here, I'll get it," Peter said. He reached around her shoulder and pulled open the door. The clattering din of the wheels on the track rose up and confronted them as they moved across the shifting iron plates between the cars.

In the dining salon the Storcks were alone at a large table and they sat down with them. The atmosphere was smoky and noisy. At the far end some students were crowded into two booths, hunched over beer and guffawing. Storck looked out the window. The vista did not change. Thorn trees and blackened shrubs covered the dry landscape. Here and there were round little houses of mud and thatch. Children in doorways waved at the train, staring, fascinated. A boy drove a group of cows along the rim of a ditch.

"You see how they live?" said Storck, pointing with his thumb. "It's no wonder so many want to come work in the mines. Economically, the black man is better off in South Africa than anywhere in Africa."

Peter's face reddened.

"But they are free here," he said.

"Freedom . . . what is freedom?" Storck asked disdainfully. "You have to eat first."

"Look, we're stopping," said Mrs. Storck.

They were pulling into a little station. The whole village had turned out to greet the train. People lined the platform, black faces upturned toward the passengers in hopes of enticing and cajoling them to buy their wares. Men and women held up carved dolls and animals, birds of steer horn, and long graceful walking sticks of hard polished mopane wood.

"But, Master! See, cheap, cheap. I give you good price," they whined and coaxed. "You like this stick? A rand, just one rand."

They moved up and down alongside the waiting train, picking out those who looked the slightest bit interested from among the smiling white passengers who watched the display from above.

Peter reached down and took a carved walking stick from an outstretched hand.

"How much?" he asked, promising himself not to buy except at one-third the asked price.

"One rand, Master," said the man.

"That's too much," said Peter, handing back the stick.

"Master, that's a good price. How much you going to give me? You say your price."

"I'll give you thirty-five."

"Master, say sixty-five."

"No, thirty-five."

They agreed at forty-five. Peter took out some change and passed it down to the man. He was smiling.

"Thank you, Master."

The passengers admired the walking stick as Peter showed it around.

Up at the forward end of the car there was some commotion as a small group of the students haggled with an old blanket-wrapped woman below. She had handed up some dolls for them and they were arguing the price. The whistle blew and the woman reached up as the train began to move.

One of the girls fumbled in her purse for some money. The people below walked along to keep up as the train rolled ahead. They began trotting. The girl finally got some change and leaned out the window holding it at arm's length toward the old woman who ran alongside.

The train was moving faster and the girl tossed the handful of coins toward the up-stretched arm of the desperate woman. The money scattered over the platform like drops of mercury.

Peter, standing at one of the aft windows, watched as the scene ahead advanced toward him. Three small boys were dangerously running beside the train. His window came abreast, and he stared unbelieving as the boys elbowed one another aside and then fell sprawling on the earth, grabbing for the rolling coins.

A Party for Raoul

When Michael came down for breakfast he smelled the aroma of freshly ground coffee and heard Nancy packing the twins off to school. They had three daughters, and Virginia, the eldest, was in her first year at Wellesley. Michael felt a sweet stab of pride whenever he remembered that.

He peered into the dining room and noted the preparations for the party they were to give that evening—cocktails, wine, and finger-food. Thirty polished glasses stood in ranks on the sideboard and a bright array of bottles—vodka, bourbon, gin and scotch—brought up the rear.

In the kitchen there was a swirl of activity.

"What time is it? You're going to miss the bus again."

"Mom, the bus is always late."

"Bye, Daddy." Hurrying lips against his cheek. The twins darted out with their books and lunch bags.

"Eleven years old," said Michael. "And they leave earlier than their father."

Nancy was just sitting down at the table.

"You're feeling guilty?" she asked.

"Don't be ridiculous."

"I wonder," she said. "You've earned the right. You don't need to don a hair shirt because you begin at ten instead of eight the way you did when you started out."

He sat down opposite her and placed two pillows of Shredded Wheat into a bowl.

"I must say I'm dreading this party," she went on, buttering her toast. "We won't know any of them except for Raoul."

Michael poured in milk and pressed the cereal down into it with the side of his spoon.

"We've met some of them," he said

"Maybe no one will show up."

"Oh, come on. It should be fun. Raoul knows interesting types."

"Isn't Raoul just about perfect?"

"No sarcasm, please."

"All right . . . it's just that every time the subject of Raoul comes up you start tearing yourself down a little. I don't like that."

"He's one of my oldest friends."

"He's not your friend. He takes advantage of you."

"No, he's a good friend. Christ, we went through high school, college, and law school together."

"Together, yes. But you're very different."

Nancy got up and started putting things away. The sun coming through the window played tricks with the fish bowl in the corner cupboard and little swirling patterns moved on the ceiling.

Michael thought about Raoul and his own career. Okay, she was right, but still . . .

"Raoul was hugely ambitious," he said. "Always wanted to make a big name for himself."

"Always out for himself."

"Maybe the quiet life doesn't appeal to everyone. I can see that."

"Is that so? Anytime you're tired of this quiet life, you know what you . . ."

"Cut it out, Nancy. I'm just thinking out loud."

He stirred his cereal. Under the table the dog struggled against his leg.

"With all his exploits," Nancy started again. "And despite his self-styled importance, Raoul has always struck me as kind of sad."

"It's not self-styled. I'm a one-horse lawyer, doing the same stuff year in, year out. He was a White House Fellow and his book was written up in The Times."

"Baloney," said Nancy. 'I like my choice, and if you were honest you'd admit you like it, too." She sat down across from him and picked up her cup. Michael raised his eyebrows and pursed his lips. Then he finished his coffee and went into the hall to put on his tweed jacket.

He picked up the newspaper and his old brief case and came back into the kitchen.

"Well, off I go again," he mumbled.

Nancy stood up and put her arms around him.

"Cheer up, grump," she said. He kissed the top of her head and loved the soft warmth of her against him.

The wind slammed the door shut behind him as he left the house. He went along Filbert Street and caught a glimpse of himself in the glass door of the apartment house at the corner. You are a respectably rumpled, rubber-soled slouch, he thought. A one-horse lawyer, and you look the part.

Divorces, contracts, wills; an occasional appearance in court. Same old stuff. This is your life, councilor. This is it.

Bullshit . . . if Nancy weren't so complacent . . .

Time for rebuttal.

Yeah? What?

Your witness. I don't know.

I could get a job with the government. Go to Washington. Maybe even go overseas like Raoul. They must need lawyers in Ghana or South America. Or anyplace.

He walked up the Divisidero hill and stopped a moment to look down at the Bay. It was a grand, crisp day. Gusts of wind rustled the few remaining dry leaves on the trees and the bite of cold brought tears to Michael's eyes as he walked along. The air had that sharp clarity brought by the sea wind. San Francisco looked wonderful. Architectural details of each house stood out—intricate cornices, and textures of stucco and shingle. He looked up into a curtained front window. A piece of African sculpture, some sort of antelope with curving horns stood framed in the brilliant glass. Raoul wants to come back to this, he said to himself. Why not? Who wouldn't?

You're very different, Nancy had said. True. Yes, Raoul had a spark, a quality of vitality that maybe he lacked. At times Michael wondered if he might just be lazy, but he quickly put that out of his mind. How could he be lazy and be where he was? He'd worked damn hard and was proud of his accomplishments. He remembered back when he and Nancy had first met and she told him that he was the most comfortable person she had ever known. He liked that, and felt better now that it came back to him. Comfortable? Did it mean *too* comfortable?

He and Raoul had rarely seen each other since law school and that last chance meeting three years ago in New York had been a disturbing one. How absolutely bizarre it was that tonight they were having a party for Raoul.

Only the weekend before he had been sitting out on the deck enjoying the Sunday Chronicle and an after-breakfast cigar. Big puffy clouds drifted across the bright blue sky. Then the phone had rung. Nancy had been in the shower and he had sworn quietly as he climbed out of the chaise-lounge.

"Hello."

"Hello, Michael."

"Raoul!"

"How are you, Michael?"

"Jesus, where are you? I thought you were back in Bolivia."

"I was, but right now I'm in New York. I'm coming out there and I've a favor to ask. I'm coming home, Michael. For good."

"To San Francisco?"

"Exactly."

Raoul wanted Michael and Nancy to call and invite a group of his friends for cocktails, people whom he had met over the years and who now lived in the Bay Area.

"I thought it would be a good way to get started again," he said. "Did you know I'm divorced?"

It had happened a few months before, and he said it was "better this way." Although Joan had the children, he saw them "frequently enough."

"Yes, I'm really moving back to San Francisco."

"What about all your travelling?"

"I don't know. People may call me. And I may get the urge again, but I've got an offer from Willard, Atkins, and McPhee. They want someone who knows his way around Washington."

"Wow. Terrific."

"Listen, I'll give you the names, Michael. About twenty-six people. Great people. Interesting people. You'll like them. Six-thirty to eight-thirty? Will you mind?"

Nancy hadn't been exactly overjoyed, but she couldn't very well object. After all, they had no plans for Friday night and despite her feelings about Raoul she knew that this friendship, which had started long before she met Michael, had a peculiar importance to him. It was beyond argument. She might pout, but she wouldn't say no.

Michael walked along Pacific Street. Strange how Raoul still considered him a good friend. He remembered back to their days at Lowell High School. Sitting in the last row in biology and drawing impossible fantasy animals on each other's notebooks. There was something exclusive about their friendship. At least, Raoul wanted it to be that way. For an eleventh grader he had some fairly snobbish attitudes. Kids he didn't like for airy reasons, teachers at whom he poked fun privately. A kind of early sick-humor, but Michael had gone along with it. We had a lot of fun, he remembered. But I was the follower. Raoul, the leader.

At six-thirty that evening Nancy, in a long skirt and potholder mittens, was putting a tray of crabmeat on toast rounds into the oven.

"Shouldn't they be here by now?" she asked. "Maybe they won't come. Wouldn't that be something?"

Michael waved his hand impatiently.

"It didn't give them much time," she said. "You call someone up and invite them for cocktails four days later . . . people are busy. I'll bet a lot of them won't even bother."

Michael looked around the kitchen and wondered if Raoul would find their life prosaic. He took in the cork-board cluttered with crayon drawings and notes cut out of magazines; the copper bottoms of frying pans hanging over the stove; the dog's bed in the breakfast room.

"One of these guys coming tonight worked with Raoul in Bolivia," he said. "I think he was with the CIA when Che Guevara was killed down there."

"Really?" Nancy was putting Wheat Thins around the edge of a cheese board.

"And let's see, that couple . . . Green, or Greeley or something. He was an administrative assistant to one of the Senators on the Watergate Committee and his wife is an artist."

Nancy was carrying the ice bucket into the living room.

"Who else?" she asked.

17

"Oh, some other lawyers. I think I know one or two of them, but they're in government mostly. And then that missionary—you know, the guy whose colleague was killed by savages in Paraguay. And his wife. Anyway, here we are, living vicariously."

"Don't start that again, Mike, or I'll walk right out of this house and you can give the goddamned party yourself."

The bell rang and the dog ran to the front door, barking loudly.

"No, Kipper. Bad dog. No, no." Michael scooped up the dachshund and opened the door.

"Well, what a reception! Hello, Michael. Anyone here yet?" Raoul, tall and urbane in a gray suit with pin stripes, stepped into the hall.

"Come in, Raoul. Come in. Sorry about the dog. He's really a sweetheart."

Raoul gripped Michael's hand.

"Michael, this is exceptionally good of you. I appreciate it." Raoul looked at his watch.

"You're the first to arrive," said Michael as Nancy came out of the kitchen.

"It's been a long time, Raoul," she said, holding out her hand.

A little cool, Michael thought. She doesn't want him to kiss her.

"Nancy, you're more beautiful every time I see you," said Raoul, ignoring her formality with a big hug.

"Come in, come in." Michael led them into the living room.

"Lovely," Raoul said. His eye ran over the large room hung with paintings. "This is why I'm coming back to San Francisco; people know how to live graciously."

"Oh, Raoul, you're such a well-traveled man. This must seem hum-drum," Nancy said, dropping on to the sofa.

"Is that irony I sense?" Raoul smiled at her.

"I don't think so, but you do get around more than most."

"I've been around, all right. A half-million miles in the last five years and out of the country four of those five."

Michael held out his hand to the liquor cabinet.

"Scotch, gin? What'll you have?"

Michael busied himself with the drinks and Nancy probed gently.

"Tell us about these people who are coming," she said.

Raoul leaned forward in his chair.

"You know how San Francisco attracts people," he began. "Everyone seems to end up here. They're just friends—people from my past. George Pelham, the missionary. I met him in South America. Quite a guy. You won't like him at first. Never smiles. We call him 'Gravity.'"

He went on, drawing a little sketch of each person. Michael listened spellbound and Nancy lounged back, catlike and imperturbable.

They talked about their children for a while, but Raoul had little to say about his own. He seemed happier listening to Nancy telling about the twins and Virginia. She chattered on about schools and tried to draw him out about his ex-wife.

Michael watched them on the couch, each facing the other with an arm thrown out along the top. Adversaries, he saw, but, gently. Maybe just defenders of different points of view.

Raoul looked at his watch and threw a questioning look at his host. It was ten after seven.

Michael didn't want to think about that chance meeting in a clothing store in Manhattan three years ago, but just now it returned to haunt and it was making him perspire. He and Virginia had been looking at Eastern colleges and they had bumped into Raoul and his daughter the morning before they returned to San Francisco.

Fathers and daughters. The girl (Patsy, wasn't it?) brought out the worst in Raoul, and Michael still felt a flush of embarrassment when he thought about it. She was half a year older than Virginia, but seemed far younger, clinging and whining. She hung back in a sulk, visibly irritated at having to share her father with these strangers.

They went to The Brass Rail for lunch. Virginia tried to talk to Patsy, but it was no use. Every effort seemed to exhaust the girl and she began to pester Raoul about other things they needed to do that day. Raoul became annoyed, barked at her, and shifted his attention to Virginia.

"What colleges did you like, Virginia?"

Virginia brightened up and responded in her usual lively way. "Wellesley, I think; maybe Connecticut College."

Patsy shifted in her seat and they all looked at the smirk of superiority on her face.

"Something wrong with Connecticut, Patsy?" Raoul asked.

"No." She shrugged her shoulders.

Virginia smiled uneasily. "Anyway, I may go to Berkeley," she said, trying bravely to smooth the awkward moment. "Not sure I want to come all the way out East."

When they left, Raoul held Michael back a moment as the girls went through the revolving door.

"Sorry, Michael," he apologized. "She's bitchy today. At times she can be a pain. It's been rough for her with me away so much."

Michael clapped him on the shoulder and they went out on the sidewalk.

The two men were alone in the living room.

"Jesus, Michael. What'd you do to me? Where *is* everyone?" Raoul had a bruised look, a vulnerability just glimpsed. It was late—ten minutes to eight—and no one had arrived. Michael shifted uneasily.

"Don't worry. They'll come." Michael wanted to hear more adventures.

"What was Bolivia like? You had a private practice then, didn't you? How did you manage to get away?"

Raoul sipped his Scotch.

"It just happened. A decision. Quick, you know. Not planned. I've discovered those decisions work out for me. You can plan and look at all the angles carefully, but the best things I've ever done have been on impulse."

Michael watched him thoughtfully. It sounded right and true, but there was something left out, something not quite honest enough.

"The world is a big exciting thing—like a circus—and I've tried to go to all the events," Raoul said. "What about you? You see things differently?"

Michael talked about his law practice and life in San Francisco. He knew he was minimizing his achievements, but somehow he wanted to paint things beige and gray. Raoul listened, anxious now and vaguely pre-occupied. Nancy came back from the kitchen.

"Well, this is cozy, I must say. Raoul, these people are your friends?"

Raoul laughed. "I feel a little stupid."

"Maybe we didn't give them enough notice," Michael offered.

"Look, if someone doesn't come in a few minutes, I'm going to take in the welcome mat and make some lamb chops for the three of us," Nancy said. "How about it?"

Raoul shrugged with his palms up. "Sure," he said. "I'm sorry."

"Well, Michael's right," she said. "There wasn't a lot of time."

"Nancy, you really invited them?" Raoul asked. "Did you call?"

"What do you think? Of course I did. You asked us to. Every last one of them. Some said they'd be here. A couple thought yes, but they had to check their calendar."

"Oh."

Raoul got up, looked questioningly, and Michael pointed down the hall.

"Second door on the right," he said.

He and Nancy sat silently, looking up every so often to search the other's face, but neither said a word.

It seemed a long time, but when Raoul returned they saw that his eyes were reddened. He was looking at Nancy.

"I'm sorry I jumped at you that way," he said. "I had no right to do that."

"No, don't worry," she said.

He put a handkerchief up to his eyes.

"Sorry," he said.

Michael waved his hand and shook his head.

"No, no."

"Ah, well, I haven't actually rented a place here yet," said Raoul. "Testing it out, you know,"

"Are you okay, buddy?"

"Yeah, I'm okay. This was kind of a feeler. Know what I mean?"

"Sure."

"I'm just upset that you went to all this trouble."

There was a sound at the door. The dog barked once and Michael went to see.

"What is it, Mike?" asked Nancy.

"Just the wind. It's really blowing out there."

Now they were alone. It was ten-thirty. Nancy turned out the lights in the living room and Michael waited for her at the foot of the stairs.

"Can you believe it?" she said. "Not one person . . ."

Michael shook his head.

"Not that I'm totally surprised," she added.

Michael turned and put his foot on the first step, and then reversed himself to face her. "Did people write in your yearbook when you graduated from high school?" he asked.

"Of course. Why?"

"You know how people wrote those funny poems, or private jokes? *Roses are red* . . . that sort of thing?"

"Sure."

"Do you know what Raoul wrote?"

Nancy shook her head.

"He wrote: *To my good friend, Michael. Your friendship has meant a great deal to me. Good luck at college.*"

"Pretty formal for an eighteen year old."

"No one else wrote anything like that."

"He was trying to be more adult than either of you really were. But it was false."

"I've never been able to get what he wrote out of my mind. And now this . . ."

"Ah, well . . ."

They stood facing each other in the darkened hall. Just enough light from the small ceiling fixture on the second floor landing illuminated their way up and Michael saw its reflection in Nancy's eyes. She reached out for his hand and they went up together.

THE TELLING

W<small>INTER GLOOM HUNG OVER</small> Brooklyn. Car headlights glimmered through late Sunday afternoon's misty rain. On the sidewalk in front of the hospital people waited silently for the bus, their backs to the wind, and shifted from one foot to the other in slow motion. The cabbies sat hunched, motors humming and windshield wipers flapping.

Liff stepped tentatively off the curb and walked across the street to Barbara's Red-Cross Luncheonette. Inside, his glasses fogged up and he pulled out a handkerchief to wipe them. Three other interns sat talking quietly. He didn't know them and slid into the next booth, but he caught the gist of their conversation. It concerned a patient who had died and the family wouldn't give permission for a post-mortem.

Liff didn't want to listen. Today's newspaper lay discarded on the seat beside him. He spread it on the table and pretended to read.

Reactions to Khrushchev Speech

> *. . . Soviet Premier Nikita Khrushchev's recent speech accusing the Western powers of violating the demilitarization clause of the Potsdam Agreement of 1945 by rearming West Germany . . . now the Soviet Union is demanding that West Berlin be demilitarized within six months . . .*

Until that moment Liff had felt just the usual vague apprehension and anxiety of a day on call at the hospital. Butterflies in his stomach were nothing new. It wasn't because of any emergencies that might come in during his shift, but more worrying about getting enough sleep. On a typical Sunday he would make ward rounds after breakfast, complete any unfinished work on the patients, and then sign out a few old charts. After lunch he would lie down and try to get a little sleep before he was called for the first admission of the day. If one came in during the afternoon he'd be able to do his work-up before supper and then hope that nothing came in after that, but it almost never happened that way. Two to four new patients a day was more like it, and if they didn't arrive during daylight it meant a busy night.

Liff had mulled it over many times, but still couldn't figure out why getting eight or nine hours of uninterrupted sleep was so fantastically important to him. Usually the butterflies began after lunch, and his post-prandial nap was never very restful. He would curl up with his eyes shut, but his mind was constantly on the telephone sitting on the desk a foot away from his head. Regardless of the success or failure of the nap his anxiety persisted and increased during the rest of the day. At times he was very clinical about it and attributed it to a release of adrenalin and a speeding up of his heart rate. As he lay there he could feel every beat, but he was more or less resigned to it and always looked forward to the dawning of the next morning when a tired euphoric feeling caught hold of him. That's when he was finally able to relax completely in the knowledge that Monday night was a night off.

But now, as he glanced at the other three interns, Liff began to despise them, especially the short eager beaver facing him, and he started to sweat. A nauseating feeling of panic seized the pit of his stomach and he could only stare vacantly at the newspaper. Why had he even come here this afternoon?

"Coffee, Doctor?"

The sallow waitress with a pencil and pad stood next to the table.

"Uh, no. Let me have a Coke, please. Small one."

She walked back to the counter.

"I'm an ace at getting autopsies," eager beaver laughed.

"Yeah, why don't you tell us about it?" another intern challenged.

"No, look—you scare them a little. You bring up heredity, you emphasize the benefit to the rest of the family."

"Yeah, yeah. Good for you, ace."

It's all they talk about, Liff thought. At lunch, supper, off duty, on dates. Always death. Death, death. Jesus.

He wanted to get up and leave, but the waitress had set the Coke before him. He drank some quickly, left the change on the table and walked out into the cold damp air again, disturbed and annoyed. After six months in this place he wondered what was to become of his life. He knew he was depressed, but maybe they were all depressed—everyone.

So, the alternatives. A career in research? No, I can't stand the endless statistical computations about esoteric biochemical data. Even reading the titles in the journals gets me down. My patients don't upset me. I'm thorough and calm, and I know most of them appreciate what I do. They like me. Okay, I can't joke and kid with them like some guys. I'm no good with the hearty approach, but the patients have confidence in me even if I'm a little aloof.

Maybe something like radiology. I wouldn't be treating sick people myself; just read x-rays.

No, I need those patients. Maybe it's wrong, but I like the feeling of importance when I run the case myself. That's one thing I've learned since starting this internship. Even when they're gravely ill I feel pretty sure of myself. Not cocky, but a real change compared with the last few years as a student. Nothing like that awful time when I was fumbling around with that drunk who had blood spurting from his radial artery. It ended well anyway with the help of the team in the ER, but I'd feel a lot cooler about handling something like that now.

Liff returned to his room in the Staff Building, sat down on the bed and peered out the window. The gray clouds formed a false ceiling over the neighborhood. Smothering. Oppressive. The street looked small and bitter.

Sundays were the worst. Down the hall someone was listening to the Philharmonic.

He lay back on his pillow and stared at the rust stained cracks above him. Goddamn this dismal place! If I had known it was going to be like this I would never have come here.

In his last year at school a venerated professor had counseled him not to pick an internship by the size of the paycheck or the newness of the hospital.

"My most valuable years were spent in rickety old hospitals with the paint coming off the walls," the professor told him. He was a thickset man who always seemed to be straining. But, he was brilliant—a principal author of the most important textbook of medicine—and every student went to him for advice.

Liff took the advice, picked his internship accordingly, and now, after half a year, the loneliness was drowning him in this realm of death and sickness, this place where the end of life came for so many of Brooklyn's broken people. Jewish shopkeepers with coronary disease, Italian laborers with cirrhosis, old grandmothers with diabetes and bedsores, knifings, shootings, accidents, psychotics, bums, beatings, abandoned kids.

It's a myth that doctors become hardened to death. It hasn't happened to me. There's a big show of nonchalance among us. Interns—self-styled experts on life who picture themselves realists. But it's all phony as hell. Our learned reactions to death are as primitive as a child's earliest imitations of its mother's speech. We're young, and we just copy the stereotyped responses of older doctors and incorporate them into our so-called professional personalities. It's just camouflage for our frightened souls and it completely falls apart when the family of the deceased patient has to be told. The death is bad enough itself, but that merely involves self-mastery and gritting your teeth. The telling is awful. The racing pulse, the nausea, the stupid words to the scared family waiting.

"I'm sorry to have to tell you . . ."

Then comes the realization, the widening of eyes and mouth, and finally the screams and tears. How can anyone ever get used to that?

Anxiety took hold whenever Liff thought about it—the one thing that could overwhelm his courage. He'd never had trouble mastering other feelings that are engendered in students during a medical course: freshman squeamishness in anatomy about the cadaver; the sight of blood; embarrassment with female patients; and the imminence of death in the moribund. You struggled with all and faced them. No particular difficulty, but this was different.

His first death had been in July on his second night on call. A stroke. He telephoned the wife.

"I'm very sorry, but I must tell you . . . that your husband didn't make it. He passed away just a few minutes ago."

It would never disappear from his thoughts. Not the clear mental image of the dangling receiver. Not the screaming as she ran into another room. It seemed audible to him even now, and it was certainly the last time he'd tried to shield himself by using the telephone. You had to face the family directly. You had to see the impact of the words in their pitiful and terrible eyes. Each time you walked away spent and exhausted and disappointed with your own inadequacy. Each telling was a horrible *faux pas*, but all the worse because of its utter necessity and its having been consciously planned.

He'd never discussed this with his fellow interns because he suspected their honesty. Why should they tell him how they felt? Besides, what could they tell him that he didn't already know? It was too embarrassing to admit weakness. A vague taboo against exhibiting irrelevant emotion loomed up.

At six he went down to supper. The dining room was cozy. Painted a light green, it was humming now with the quiet laughter of the usual Sunday evening crowd. A mixture of people who were on call and others in sport clothes who'd had the weekend off, so the somber atmosphere of weekdays was brightened a little by a measure of relaxation and contented lounging.

Liff sat down with two foreign doctors whom he knew vaguely. One was an Indonesian girl, a pediatric resident. She was striking, her black hair done in a long braid that wound forward over her shoulder. The other was a Greek surgeon who was repeating a surgical residency so that he could practice his specialty in the United States. He was about forty, and quite affable despite his frustrating experience with the need for a second education.

"Busy?" the Greek asked with a grin. Friendly . . . in the way of the hospital family.

The norm was to act cheerful and happy, whatever the trying circumstances. It wasn't exactly forced. In fact, there was a great deal to be said for it. Even if the spirit wasn't completely sincere, it was contagious and made others comfortable, but just now Liff didn't feel much like responding.

"Not bad, not bad," he sighed, for want of something more inspired to say.

He began eating rather hurriedly. The other two had apparently been engaged in some sort of personal talk and Liff sensed his intrusion. He felt an awkward desire to express his sensitivity to foreign cultures, especially downtrodden ones. He always had the urge to become involved with exotic people, but never seemed able to cross the gulf between his mute dreams and conversational reality.

"This place is wonderful for experience," said the Greek to no one in particular. "We never have something like it in Greece for interns."

They spoke lightly about the hospital for a few minutes. Liff began to feel better and made a few pungent remarks about the hospital's administration. They all laughed. Liff wondered about the relationship between the other two. She is really charming, he thought. A little young for the Greek. He seems almost like a father. They sat around over coffee for fifteen minutes. Liff looked at his watch, stood up and excused himself. They waved to him, smiling.

He went up to his room and tried to sleep. The food had made him drowsy, but he tossed and turned, punching his pillow into more comfortable shapes. Several times he fell asleep, but was awakened by the telephone when the nurse on his ward had to ask him something about one or another of the patients. At midnight he got up and read the newspaper for twenty minutes until he couldn't follow the print on the pages. Then he flicked out the light and fell asleep, dreaming weird fantasies in which he and the Indonesian girl were swimming in the pool before the Taj Mahal.

At four-thirty the jangling of the phone wrenched him from his agitated rest. He leaned over on one elbow and picked up the receiver.

"Doctor Liff, this is the nurse on C-1. You have an admission—myocardial infarction in shock."

"How's he look?"

"You'd better come right over."

"Yeah, thanks."

He turned on the light, and went to the sink to brush his teeth, a little ritual which helped him wake up. He did this every time he had to admit a new patient at night. After dressing he closed the door to his room quietly and went down the hall to the bathroom where he urinated sleepily.

Outside he walked briskly along the four blocks to C building. It had stopped raining and a hard wind blew down through the denuded skeleton-like trees along the curb. Their lower limbs creaked only slightly while the slender terminal branches slapped furiously back and forth.

Liff, hands in pockets, shivered in his thin uniform. He observed his moving shadow lengthen and then suddenly disappear with each succeeding lamppost.

As he passed the various hospital buildings, each one standing several massive stories above the sidewalk, he speculated on the severity of his patient's heart attack. He shared a philosophic realization with most interns that the death of a patient shortly after admission to the hospital meant a brief note on the chart and a minimal amount of lost sleep. There are all kinds of coronaries and they vary from mild to catastrophic. On nights like these he was dimly aware of a moral dilemma in which the desire for a peaceful eight-hour rest contended with his conscience that fought off certain vague musings that the case might come to a quick end. He wasn't ashamed about this because he never had truly hoped for it, but the play of ideas was usually present in his mind on dark nights as he walked to the hospital wards to meet an unknown patient. It was as if the very absence of light allowed the disquieting notions entrance into his thoughts. Nonetheless, the element of fate inherent in how new patients were admitted to the various wards of the hospital according to a pre-arranged rotation schedule absolved him from brooding. It was all rather matter-of-fact.

Three ambulances from smaller Brooklyn hospitals were parked in the narrow concrete yard outside the Emergency Door. Liff glanced at them and mentally cursed hospitals which turned away patients due to *no beds available*, the usual excuse given by the referring hospitals.

Several little groups of tired people sitting on long brown benches looked up at him blankly as he walked through the ugly waiting room illuminated by grimy incandescent fixtures placed along the walls. He wondered if an anxious looking middle-aged woman sitting alone might be the wife of his patient. She was short, and faded looking, but there was something—perhaps it was her dress, or her hair—that made him think she had probably once been pretty, or even beautiful. He couldn't tell. Her face was bent down, inclined toward her folded hands.

Liff's foot kicked a dusty newspaper lying in the middle of the floor as he turned the corner into the corridor leading to C-1.

The nurse handed him the chart and walked along with him to the curtained room beyond.

"It's Paul Hnilicka. Do you know him?" she asked.

"No."

"Paul's had several admissions over the past two years. He's one of the plumbers here in the hospital. Patient of Doctor Sand's. He was just discharged about a month ago after his third coronary. He looks terrible."

They stood by the bed. A distressed middle-aged man lay in it, conscious, but gasping oxygen through a facemask. Liff smiled reassuringly at him as he felt the faint rapid pulse at the wrist. The skin was pale, sweaty and faintly blue. Johnson, the emergency room intern, was stooped over a cuff on the other arm taking the patient's blood pressure. He took off his stethoscope and moved back, then came around the bed and stood quietly behind Liff.

"Sixty over zero," he said quietly. "And now he's all yours."

"Thanks."

"I've got some Aramine running in that bottle," Johnson said, motioning toward the IV infusion hanging from a steel pole by the bedside.

"Thanks," said Liff, watching his colleague walk back down toward the emergency room.

The nurse came up alongside. "The woman in the waiting room is the wife," she said. "Doctor Johnson spoke to her when they brought him in, but that was about twenty minutes ago."

"I'll talk to her."

Liff went over and introduced himself. The woman grabbed his sleeve. "He's all I've got, Doctor. Please save him!"

"We'll do everything we can, Mrs. Hnilicka. He's seriously ill . . . a very bad heart attack again. We'll go all out, but you have to realize . . . he's pretty sick right now."

Factual questions, he told himself. Maneuver her away from emotions.

"What happened tonight?" he asked.

Typical story. Some mild pain after dinner gradually worsening during the evening. The patient tried to sleep, but the pain got worse and was unrelieved by his nitroglycerin tablets. He began to sweat, vomited several times, and then complained to his wife about the pain. By the time he had reached the hospital, he was in agony.

Liff went back into the curtained room. He hooked up the electrocardiograph to the patient and studied the paper tracing as it came out of the machine. In addition to evidence of old healed disease in the heart muscle he noted new changes and up-swept lines that meant recent and more acute damage. He tore off the long strip and put it in his pocket.

"Are you having much pain, Mr. Hnilicka?" he asked the man.

"No. The shot the nurse gave me seems to be helping. It's much better," he said grimly. He was very still and seemed afraid of moving.

Liff checked the blood pressure. It was falling.

He went out to the nurse's desk again and got a tray marked *Cut-Down* from the cabinet over the sink.

"Can you help me with this?" he asked the nurse. She was preparing some medication for another patient.

"Sure thing."

They went back to the bedside. While Liff put on sterile gloves and prepared some surgical instruments on the tray the nurse cleansed an area of the man's skin near the left ankle with some orange antiseptic. Liff injected a local anesthetic, made a little incision, and slipped a thin plastic tube into a vein that he opened with a tiny scissors. He attached the tube to another IV infusion, bandaged the whole area and took his gloves off. After a few minutes he checked the blood pressure again. It had come up a few points.

"That'll help some," he told the nurse. "Will you keep an eye on it while I write a few notes in the chart?"

He went out to the desk and began writing his admission notes in the usual stark and abbreviated phrases. The several forms that had to be filled out he did more or less mechanically.

He was thinking about the wife. She would take it hard. The poor fellow was going to die despite everything. His life was slipping away rapidly and would be gone soon. Liff felt very alone. The sterility and glare of the emergency ward and the bareness of the little metal desk in front of him did not alter an almost palpable uneasiness that seemed to lurk in the place. It made him feel homesick and queasy.

It was almost six. He picked up the telephone and made a call to his resident. They spoke briefly about the details of the case and agreed that Professor Sand, the cardiologist, ought to be called. The resident said he would ask Sand to come over.

Liff wrote a few orders for the nurse and returned to the curtained bedside. He felt a bit easier knowing that the Professor was coming over. If the fellow died while Sand was there Liff could retreat to the background since Mr. Hnilicka was one of the Professor's special cardiac patients. Although Sand spent most of his time in teaching and research he had a few patients such as this man whom he followed himself in the outpatient Cardiac Clinic. Sand was an unusual man for a Professor. Unmarried, he lived about two blocks from the hospital and spent most of his time working. He took his meals in the hospital dining room with the interns and residents and could be found in his laboratory almost every night until one or two in the morning. Despite his eminence, and the fact that the younger doctors looked upon him as another Sir William Osler, Sand was kindly and generous and had a sparkling wit that he shared with everyone.

Liff's spirit rose at the thought. Warmed by this promise of fatherly protection, he drew back the curtain and looked down at his dying patient. Unconscious, there was little to distinguish him from a cadaver now except the irregular breathing. The skin was cold and mottled. Liff tried to get a blood pressure reading, but there was no pulse. The nurse came in and stood alongside. Silently, they watched. At last, a convulsion seized the whole body, the muscles contracting involuntarily. There were two gasps, and then no movement.

Rigid.

Stillness.

Liff put his stethoscope on the man's chest.

Nothing.

He stepped back and stared at the man who lay dead before him. Alive . . . dead, he thought. Just the beating of a heart.

They walked out of the room. A tall gray haired man in a white coat was coming from the emergency entrance toward them. The wife waited against the wall, wide-eyed and apprehensive. Liff approached the tall man and stopped him in the middle of the hall.

"Doctor Sand, it's Paul Hnilicka. He just expired," said Liff.

"All right. Let's go into the room."

They passed the wife again and went to the bedside where the dead man lay. Doctor Sand drew back the sheet and looked at the corpse.

"What happened?' he asked.

Liff repeated the essential details as he had heard them from the wife. Sand listened and stared at the bed from time to time. He looked at the EKG tracing that Liff had pulled from his pocket.

"You did everything that you could. He wouldn't have lasted another three months at the rate he'd been deteriorating," said Sand. "I've known Paul and his wife for several years now. There were times when I wouldn't have believed he'd make it, but he surprised me. He was a nice man."

He thought for a moment.

"Let's go out now," he said.

Liff followed him into the hall. Sand walked toward the wife leaning against the wall.

"It's all over," he said quietly.

Her eyes widened and strained in their dark-ringed sockets. She looked wild.

"It had to happen sooner or later this way, Mrs. Hnilicka. We all knew it."

"Oh, no, no, no!" she cried. Tears streaked her ravaged face. She sank to the floor and beat the tiles with her fists.

Sand crouched beside her and held her shoulder. The woman turned and looked at him.

"Come, Mrs. Hnilicka. Let me . . ."

He and Liff reached under her arms and helped her into a chair. She buried her face in her hands. Sand said something to the nurse who walked over to a cabinet filled with medicines.

Liff watched the scene. They were calling a relative to come and pick her up. Sand was soothing her with words—poised, even in this situation. Liff sat down at the desk to fill out more forms. They took the woman into another room and Sand went with her, kneading her with kindness. Suddenly it was very quiet. Liff finished his notes, put a code number on the front sheet of the chart and wrote after it *Arteriosclerotic heart disease, infarction of the myocardium.* He attached all the forms with a paper clip and placed the completed chart on the desk. He felt relieved that the wife was gone.

There was nothing to do now. He could go to breakfast. Thank God for Sand.

The sun hurt his eyes as he stepped out onto the pavement. The sky was sparkling blue and cloudless except for the curling white smoke coming from the tall chimney of the hospital heating plant. People were beginning to arrive for work. Two young nurses scurried past him, their starched uniforms making soft creaky whispering sounds.

"Morning, Doctor."

So cheerful.

"Hi."

He walked on, yawning. How tired . . .

Today's Monday . . . I'm off tonight.

THE HOTEL OF THE
ISLE OF DREAMS

THE SCORPION STRUCK SWIFTLY, piercing Fred Heath's index finger. A shock of intense pain shot up his arm and he pulled back, losing his balance and dropping to the boat's deck.

"Fred!" Vicki stood over him, her face ashen.

"I'm ok."

"My God . . ."

He winced and struggled to his feet.

He'd seen the creature scuttle back to the end of the bench that ran along the outside of the cabin and then disappear into a crack between the boards.

A drop of blood oozed out of the ragged little hole in his finger. That a scorpion sting might be dangerous passed quickly from his mind. More, he was caught by a dreamy awareness that this probably happened often in the tropics.

And how strange it was—an attack by nature in balmy air with bright sun and the blue-green sea all around them. And the palm trees, too, some of them dotted with flashes of white that he knew were pelicans roosting up there.

""I'm alright . . . I'm alright." He sat back on the bench. "I'll take an antibiotic."

The craft was tossing quite a bit and he gazed out over the churning wake toward the receding mainland.

Carlos, the young boatman who had been silent ever since they'd left the marina, called over to him.

"Everything okay?"

"A scorpion . . ."

"*Oh, Dios mio!*"

"I want to take a pill. Do you have some water?"

Carlos reached down and passed an unopened plastic bottle.

Fred searched in his bag and found his medical kit.

"Shouldn't you wash it?" Vicki asked.

Fred nodded and put his hand over the side. The salt water was cool and soothing.

They had rarely ventured far from Minneapolis, but both of them knew it was high time. For months they had talked about wanting a change. Maybe even a new sort of life.

"So much for paradise," Vicki said.

"I'll be okay. We said we were up for an adventure."

He popped one of the white pills into his mouth and drank from the bottle.

Fred knew very little about scorpions, but he wasn't going to let it spoil things. "Look around," he said. "This *is* paradise."

A flock of terns came darting in and he watched them dive-bomb into the waves. There were splashes all around, silvery forms arcing out of the water.

When Vicki had heard from friends about the possibility of retiring south of the border, Fred was more than intrigued. He was a busy general surgeon, not quite sixty, but slowing down and tired, and he was hoping for something different. Right off, Central America had seemed an attractive choice—not too far away, and less expensive than Europe.

He leaned back against the peeling painted surface of the cabin and looked at his wife. She was calmer now and sitting again in the plastic deck chair. Her face was turned to the sun and in a crisp white piqué dress edged in blue she had a fresh, even elegant poise that seemed oddly out of place in the vibrating, battered, and grimy old craft. The long ends of a thin white scarf covering her hair fluttered in the wind.

She has an artist's eye, Fred mused. A sense of style . . . even sitting in an open boat like this.

He put a Band-Aid on the wound. The spot was tender when he touched it. It would take a few days, he knew.

Doggedness had carried him through medical school and the grinding years of surgical residency, but he enjoyed his work and his practice was successful and rewarding. Still, by sixty-five he would no longer want to be in the operating room, so it wasn't too early to begin considering the future.

At first the concept was vague, nothing more than a fantasy. The Central America in guidebooks was colorful and interesting, but Fred, in his usual determined fashion, had to know more. He read broadly and deeply about the history of the area, and both of them sought out people who had traveled a lot. It took awhile, especially to make the arrangements needed to cover Fred's practice, but now it was before them.

Carlos was smiling. He wore a greasy yachting cap and tattered shorts, balancing easily in a wide barefoot stance at the wheel.

"In a few minutes, *Señor*, we'll see the island. *Isla Soleada*—you will like it."

Fred yawned and fingered the boat's chipped paint. It was the time of year when the Indians burned the dry grass and the acrid scent of smoke that had hovered over the port and the surrounding hills was evident even out here on the gulf. The mid-morning sun had begun to beat down through the haze with sultry intensity. A few fishing boats were already returning to port.

"There!" Carlos yelled.

He had taken one hand off the helm and was pointing ahead toward the far shore where a peninsula formed the other side of the gulf. Against the blur of distant mountains a small rocky island was beginning to emerge as a distinct form.

"*Isla Soleada?*" Fred asked.

"*Sí*," said Carlos. "*Sí*, but, I have a different name."

"What do you call it?"

"*Isla de Sueños.*"

"Dreams," Vicki said.

"*Sí.*"

"Oh, I love it."

"Ah, it is only my idea."

They saw, and smiled. This was the piece of their trip that had most strongly drawn them. After a few days in Mexico to see the ruins, followed by a few more in Guatemala to see the markets and more ruins, this final stay at the fishing camp on the island would be the best part. Isolated, quiet, and, if the reports were correct, with stunning natural beauty, they were hoping it held the finest chance for something extraordinary—something transformational.

"You will be the only people at the hotel," said Carlos.

Vicki looked at Fred and then at Carlos.

"No other guests," he explained. "All of them left yesterday. Just the *gringo—un norteamericano—Señor* Mathews and his wife."

A line of pelicans came gliding silently toward the boat, their enormous wings holding them marvelously just inches above the waves.

"Who is Mathews?" Fred asked.

Carlos took off his cap and wiped his forehead with the back of his hand.

"He is a friend of Don Guillermo," he answered, replacing the cap. "He wants to buy the hotel from him."

"Don Guillermo must be Willy Jones," Fred said softly to Vicki. They knew of Willy Jones from a friend of theirs who had stayed on the island. Jones was a hard-drinking expatriate lawyer who had lived for years on the island with a common-law wife named Lupe and their little son. Jones had put up some cabins and made a living by running a simple establishment for the few guests who came for the fishing.

"Willy Jones is selling the hotel?" Fred asked. "When will that be?"

"I don't know, *Señor*," Carlos shrugged. "But he is leaving. He wants to go back to Chicago."

Fred looked back at the long trail of smoke hanging in the still air. It was almost noon and only the small breeze created by their passage gave relief from the heat.

The island lay just ahead. Two fishing boats were moored in the cove, and among palms and mango trees they could see low wooden buildings. High over the island a great black frigate bird, its forked tail spread wide, circled slowly in the cloudless air. As they came closer to the beach, Fred saw two men wearing sombreros scraping the hull of an upturned dinghy. Another man in bathing trunks stood in the water waving. Carlos cut the engine and, as the boat bobbed and rocked slowly toward the beach, this man waded out to them.

"Hello, Heaths," he called. "Welcome to *Isla Soleada*."

He held the side of the boat as Carlos dropped anchor.

"Ralph Mathews," he said, extending a hand. "I'm kind of running things while Willy is in town."

Mathews was about fifty, deeply tanned, and athletic. He helped them climb down and they waded ashore.

"How's the fishing?" Fred asked.

"Fabulous. You'll love it, Doctor," Mathews replied. "We'll get you out there in the morning. Carlos will take you in the outboard and you can troll for mackerel, cabrilla, grouper—anything you want."

They walked up the beach toward the buildings.

"Carlos," Mathews called back. "Bring the suitcases up to Number Three . . . *por favor . . . gracias.*"

Mathews grinned broadly at them.

"Do you know Spanish?" he asked.

"A little, from high school," said Vicki.

"I've tried to learn," said Mathews. "But they understand me anyway, so I figure . . . what the hell."

He laughed and they followed him up the walk to the office.

"Willy went into town," he said, explaining that *town* meant the country's capital—an hour away by small airplane. "He won't be back until day after tomorrow, but between me and my wife, and Lupe, we ought to be able to fix you some good meals. Lupe's a darn good cook when we can find her."

He gave a short little laugh and Vicki nudged Fred, who pretended not to notice. As they entered the small dim office cluttered with cardboard boxes and unopened cases of beer, someone came in from the back. It was Mathews' wife, Peggy. She was an attractive woman somewhere between youth and middle age—strands of gray in her long black hair—but her movements were easy and graceful. Her loose caftan and necklace of small silver bells gave her a cosmopolitan flair.

"We're going to buy the place from Willy," said Mathews. "Right now he's ironing out the details of the transfer of property. The government complicates things if the sale is to another American."

"How long have you been here?" Vicki asked.

"We came four months ago," said Peggy, looking briefly at her husband. There was an abstracted air about her. "I guess that seems like a long time, don't you think?"

"Peggy's a city girl," said Mathews. "But she's getting used to the island." His smile was hopeful, and quick.

"We have a few problems," said Peggy. "Lupe is never here when we need her, but I guess things will work out."

Vicki signed and wrote their address in the guest book.

Mathews perused what she'd written. "Well, you doctors get around," he said. "And by the way, now that you're here feel free to wander about. There's plenty to see. Get comfortable. I'll tell you more about the place later on."

He led them to a thatched cabin in a clump of banana trees. The suitcases were already on the screened porch.

"Nice luggage," he said, pointing to the two leather bags.

He showed them where everything was in their room—the towels, the switch for the overhead fan.

"We've got bug spray if you need it; and you can drink the water from the tap. Come on down to the bar when you're ready and we'll have some lunch."

He left them, and Vicki tossed herself down on the bed. She waited until Mathews' footsteps died away and then began to giggle.

"Howdy, folks," she mimicked. "I may not know any of their language, but I sure can make 'em work for me."

"I get it, I get it," said Fred. "But let's just have a good time. I'm not reforming the world."

"That Peggy seemed eager to talk to new people."

"She was being friendly."

"Maybe."

Fred changed into a bathing suit and stepped outside. It was very hot in the direct sun and he leaned against the trunk of a palm tree looking out at the water. Mathews was down at the beach gesturing at the two men working on the boat, but Fred could hear him plainly.

"I want you to paint it. Paint, you understand? After you scrape it, you've got to paint it. You know . . . paint!"

He was flapping his hand up and down and the men smiled sheepishly. Mathews spoke louder, but finally shrugged and walked up the beach.

The bar of the hotel faced the sea. It was an open porch sheltered overhead by palm thatch and from the shaded recess Fred peered out at the brilliant world outside. He took in the boats anchored there, the sound of pebbles being tumbled by waves on the beach, and the immense spectacle of blue-green water, fragrant air, and dazzling light. Vicki, looking very appealing in her apricot bathing suit, sat in a wicker chair reading a mystery.

"Well, do you like it?" he asked quietly.

She shook her head and dropped her gaze back to her book.

"We wanted something quiet, didn't we? At least, I did," he said.

"It's grubby," she mumbled. "And Mathews gives me the creeps. I feel sorry for his wife."

No, it wasn't Vicki's kind of place. Fred scanned the unpainted walls of the building and the torn screens. The whole place had a ramshackle look, stricken by the sun and beaten down by the tropics. And yet, one could see that it had possibilities. The setting was lovely.

Mathews and Peggy were fixing lunch, moving back and forth from the kitchen with plates and napkins and silverware, but they seemed awkward and uncomfortable in their roles as hotelkeepers.

"I'm afraid this is just a makeshift meal," said Peggy. "But Lupe will be back for supper."

The four of them sat down to sandwiches and iced tea. Mathews was telling how he'd started a business in Arizona, had built it up, and then recently sold it.

"I made out real well," he said. "Now it's time to retire."

The bravado was annoying, but Fred sensed beneath it a man unguarded and vulnerable.

"Yeah, I've got the capital," Mathews went on. "Although, I don't know if I mentioned it, but we're going to sell off part of the shares here—that's so we can fix the place up."

He put down his sandwich. "This is my idea of paradise," he said. "We can be almost completely self-sufficient here."

Peggy sipped her iced tea looking out across the gulf. She turned and smiled at her husband. He had it all figured out. She had confidence in him.

"We know what repairs need to be done," she said. "It's really just a matter of having enough guests to keep things running, and then we can spend the rest of our time, you know, scuba diving and living."

"Sounds ideal," said Fred. "But you said before that the government makes things complicated for Americans. Won't that be a problem?"

Mathews shook his head. "Money talks in this country." He held up two fingers and placed them side-by-side. "Willy is like this with some powerful people."

They were open about the friction with Lupe. "She's definitely a problem for us," Mathews said. "And she doesn't want to go back to Chicago with Willy. We'll have to get rid of her as soon as we take over."

"She's angry that Willy is selling out and jealous of us," Peggy said. "But she won't go to the States with him—and she thinks she owns the place."

"That must be very difficult," Vicki imagined.

"Yeah," said Mathews. "We have no choice. First thing, she goes."

"How much are the shares you're selling? What percentage does the buyer get?" Fred asked.

Willy wanted $200,000 for the hotel and Mathews was willing sell off five percent for $10,000. "I'd like to sell ten percent of it, either to one or two parties," he explained. "And that would include a free four-week stay every year. And, of course, a proportionate amount of any profit we turn."

Fred sat forward in his chair, chin resting on clasped hands.

"Has anyone bought yet?" Vicki asked.

"I've got a couple of friends who'll be interested as soon as things are final," Mathews replied. "But if it appeals to you, let me know before you leave. Things will move along, and I can keep you posted about the details."

"Sounds interesting," said Fred.

As they were talking, a slender brown girl in her twenties had come into the bar. She held a chubby little boy by the hand.

"*Buenas tardes*," she greeted them, smiling at Vicki who replied in Spanish.

"Where have you been, Lupe?" Mathews asked, affecting a light-hearted tone. He was afraid of her.

"To see my mother. She needed me."

Mathews explained that there was a village on the other side of the island. "Lupe has her family there," he said.

Peggy rose to clear away the dishes and Lupe sat down at the table with them. The boy reached over for a piece of bread and she picked it up for him.

"He is always eating," she said proudly. "He's so fat."

Fred was struck by her poise and easy manner. It was obvious that she belonged here, and that this was her home. She was no intruder. When she realized that Vicki understood Spanish she ignored Mathews completely.

Fred's siesta was restless and disturbed. A fly buzzed in the room, assaulting the screen with short tapping rushes. He looked over at Vicki. Her face was turned away and her side moved with a slow and regular swell, but when he rolled from the bed to tiptoe out she woke up.

"Where are you going?" she asked.

"I'll just walk around."

Vicki sat up. "Maybe I'll go talk to Peggy," she said.

Tiny waves lapped the beach and a gentle breath of warm air barely moved a few palm fronds. Mathews was lying in a hammock strung between two trees in front of the office. One leg hung out and dragged in the sand. He was awake and motioned to Fred.

"Too hot to sleep, eh?"

"I slept a little," said Fred.

"It's a great custom, the siesta."

"Hard for Americans to adapt, I guess."

"Want to see the island?"

"Sure."

Mathews swung his leg down and stood. He yawned and stretched.

"Get a drink first," he suggested. They stopped for a glass of water in the dark little office and then Mathews led Fred along the beach and up the side of a hill behind the building. The grass was brown and little thorns scratched their legs. They went through an orchard of orange and lemon trees and then up a steeper slope planted with corn. A man chopping weeds with a machete stood up to look at them. Mathews waved and the man gave a small return gesture.

"Look at that guy," said Mathews. "Toiling away in the hot sun like that all day long."

"Hard work," Fred agreed.

The path was rocky and narrower and Fred stopped to catch his breath. Turning, he looked back and gazed out at the broad expanse of blue water. The view was exceptional and he felt enormously happy. What a wonderful place, he thought. Could I live here, spend the rest of my life here?

Impossible.

Mathews had gone ahead and was almost at the summit. Fred waved and resumed the climb, sweating profusely, but exhilarated. Mathews pointed to a large flat boulder that formed a natural ledge.

"We'll perch there and take in the view."

For several minutes they sat quietly watching the continual circling far above the sea of vultures and frigate birds that wheeled slowly through the air.

"That worker down there," Mathews said. "Some life, eh?"

Fred looked at him, and nodded in agreement.

"I was born poor, too," Mathews went on. "Never knew my old man."

"Oh?"

"Yeah, he got a hard-on for some little slut and left my mother right after he found out she was pregnant with me."

"Terrible," said Fred, shaking his head.

"Yeah, but I've always had a dream about living on an island," said Mathews. "A quiet place, away from everything. I mean, what's it all for if you can't enjoy it?"

The boats down in the cove looked very small. The light breeze felt good on Fred's sweating face.

"What did you do before you came down here?" he asked.

"I've worked as long as I can remember—everything from mowing lawns and caddying to dishwashing and waiting on tables in college. Then I went into the Army—the infantry. Stayed in for twenty and came out a major. Korea, the Philippines, Japan, Greece, Washington, the Congo. When I got out I set up a small business in Arizona making plastic fittings for chemistry labs. Sold it, and now here I am."

Mathews was friendly and direct. There was a boyish quality about him that put Fred in mind of pals he had known long ago. Here on the hill he seemed more open than he'd been back at the hotel.

"How about you?"

"Oh, the usual thing for a doctor—a lot of work, too. Long training, long hours. When I think about all the years I've been in medicine I can hardly believe it."

Fred began to feel a small sense of uneasiness as if there were some secret between them, some collusion that he didn't understand. Mathews lay back on one elbow.

"I never thought about an island," said Fred. "If I've had a fantasy it's probably been of a cabin on a lake. But I can see that this would be pretty wonderful, too."

"Yes, and have you achieved it? Do you have the cabin?"

"It's only an idea. Not very practical."

"Why not?"

"I don't know."

He paused to see if Mathews was interested, and Mathews was looking at him, not smiling, but serious.

"I'd like to have time to digest things," Fred went on. "Time to assimilate my experiences, to make them a part of me. That's pretty difficult when things go by so damned fast. Up at six, rounds at seven, operate at eight, sandwich at twelve, dictate reports until one, office until five, emergencies at night, sleep deprivation—all that, and more. But I'm not complaining. I wouldn't be doing it if I didn't like it."

"Yeah, I know. I wouldn't want to be a doctor," Mathews laughed. "Anyway, I have a theory. It's women who run the show. If you left it up to most men they'd have their island or their cabin. Women want everything and we go along with it. That's what happened with my first wife. Always after me to do something, to be somebody."

"How long have you and Peggy been married?"

"Only a year. She's terrific. She's willing to try anything once," he laughed. "She paints. This is the perfect place for her. Yeah, we're getting along fine."

"Children?"

"One boy. Hardly ever see him. He lives with his mother in L.A. She's gotten to him—about what happened, I mean. He doesn't want to see me."

"I'm sorry. That's too bad."

"No, just the way things worked out."

Vicki found Peggy in a large screened room that she used as a studio just off the bar. It faced a broad stretch of sand with cactus and palm trees twenty or thirty yards beyond. The smells of paint and turpentine were in the air and Peggy stood at an easel.

"May I come in?"

Peggy turned and smiled. "Sure, you can even have a look."

Vicki came closer.

"Oh, my," she said. "You're really good. Yes, it's you, of course."

"Yeah, one version of me." Peggy stepped away and looked critically at her image. "I'm rather pleased with it, but I need to get out and paint more of what's here on the island. I think this is more the *me* from before. From before coming here."

"I'm sure it's a big change."

Peggy looked away for a moment, and then came back quickly to Vicki's face with an expression that hinted of acknowledgment and of acceptance.

"I do love it here," she said. "But you're right. It is different."

"Where were you before?"

"I grew up in New York, but we moved to L.A. when I was in high school. So, mostly L.A."

"Were you pretty involved in the art world?"

"Yeah, for sure, and I'm not giving that up, but a change is good for me. A new perspective."

"Running a hotel?"

"Ah, well . . . we'll have to see."

"Of course, it's a small hotel."

"What do you mean?"

"Well, if you had tons of guests, that'd be pretty demanding."

"Oh, sure. But it won't be like that."

"I guess you'll have more freedom and time for your painting," Vicki observed.

"I'm counting on it."

They were silent for a few moments.

Peggy put her brush down and wiped her hands. "I'll get us something cold," she said.

Vicki looked around the room at other paintings that leaned against the wall, some abstract and dark, but others that realistically captured the brilliant midday light of the island.

When Peggy returned with lemonade they sat quietly on low chairs at a bridge table. A little breeze had come up and it was very pleasant and quiet.

"What do you do in Minneapolis? Do you work?"

"I do interior decorating," Vicki said. "But I'm tapering down and have just a few clients. I guess you could say I'm nearly retired, and I'm very happy with that."

"But the doctor is still working, right?"

"Yes, he's quite active."

"How old are you?"

"I'm fifty-nine."

"Yeah."

"And you?"

"Forty-five."

They both laughed.

"Does that make a difference?" Vicki asked.

"I don't know. Maybe we all have to think ahead."

"You and Ralph . . . how long . . ?"

"We've been married a year. Seems like yesterday."

"You and he . . ?"

"Oh, we get along fine."

"That's good."

During dinner Fred felt more pain in his hand and he looked at his forearm. A red streak had developed and it was tender to the touch.

"I'll increase the Cipro dose," he told Vicki. "I feel okay—no fever yet, no swollen glands."

Later, they sat quietly on their little porch.

"I don't like the idea of us being here, and you with that infection, and we're so far away from any help," she said.

"I'll be okay. I'm not worried."

"I'll have to admit that it's pretty."

"The setting?"

"Yes, and the possibilities."

"Are you kidding? I thought you didn't like it."

"It's Mathews I don't like."

"You talked to Peggy?"

"I did."

"What's she like?"

"Interesting. Likeable. She's strong, and flexible."

"I figured. He's pretty different, but I guess they're into this."

"I don't know."

"She has doubts?"

"Nothing explicitly admitted, but it would be a big change for her."

"But when you said you think it has possibilities, what are you driving at?"

"I'm just saying that it has possibilities."

Fred pondered, and remained silent.

More of a breeze had come up and he went into the room to get a jacket. When he came back, Vicki said, "We could do it."

"Do what?"

"Buy it."

"You're crazy."

"I'm not crazy, and I'm not talking about running a hotel."

"You mean . . ."

". . . a place for us, a home, a different scene."

"You're kidding."

"Don't be so sure."

"Wait—we just arrived this morning, and you're already . . ."

She leaned back in her chair and stretched out her arms. "It wouldn't be any crazier than their idea."

Fred knew he was actually less startled than he appeared. The thought had certainly occurred to him. Then he burst out laughing.

"Wow, great minds think alike, don't we?"

"I know you, Fred Heath. I know how your mind operates."

The fishing next morning was as good as Mathews had promised. The inflamed streak on Fred's arm was fading, and the local tenderness almost gone. All sorts of fish rose high up enough in the waves so that he and Vicki could see their red and orange spots and spiny fins just below the water's sparkling and luminous surface. Within two hours there were eight large sleek and shining mackerel, snapper, and grouper on the floor of the dinghy, and Carlos headed back to the island.

Mathews took photographs of them standing on the beach with their catch, and then he and Peggy swam with them. Afterwards they lay on the hot sand until lunch.

"What are you thinking?" Vicki asked. They had agreed on a siesta, but now, in their cabin, she lay on her side, cupped hand supporting her chin, and let the question hang in the air between them.

"I'm not," said Fred. "I'm determined to sleep."

"I mean about this place—we should talk about it."

"I don't think you're serious. Or are you?"

"I'm serious enough."

"Okay, spell it out," Fred said, sitting up. "You're amazing, but I shouldn't be surprised. You're talking about some kind of commitment? You think we're ready even to consider that?"

"You know, you're actually the one who's been kind of fixated on this for months. All those books . . . you can't deny . . ."

"I don't deny anything, but what about this? Is it even feasible?"

"I don't know," she said. "I'd like to pump Mathews a little more—maybe tonight after dinner. But what we really should do is talk seriously to Willy Jones when he gets here. We'd have to corner him and get him away from Mathews for half an hour. That may not be easy. Mathews is like glue. He'll be around us, and around Willy, constantly. I could be wrong, but that's how I see it."

"You mean we'd take Willy Jones aside—assuming that's even possible—and ask him lots of questions, and then tell him we're kind of interested? Is that what you have in mind?"

"We have nothing to lose."

"Hey," Fred laughed. "I'm glad I'm married to you."

In the evening after dinner the two couples sat on the porch in front of the bar talking about the memorably delicious fresh fish they'd just eaten and how the original Indians had lived off the land. In the balmy night the island seemed turned in on itself. Crickets embroidered the stillness with crisp traceries of sound and they watched bats swooping and banking in the air beyond the porch.

"How are you going to manage here, not knowing Spanish, not being able to talk to the people," Vicki asked Mathews cautiously.

"That won't be a problem," he replied. "I know enough to get by."

"And the isolation," Vicki suggested tentatively, looking over at Peggy.

"I try to take things as they come," Peggy said. She talked about the beauty of the island and the peace. "When we got married I knew we'd be doing something like this. For Ralph it's kind of a dream come true, and I'm more ready for a change than I ever imagined."

Mathews went into the bar to fix some drinks. Fred wondered what Peggy's life had been like before meeting Mathews and becoming his wife. She had married rather late, and had probably been fairly independent.

"But do you miss the excitement of the city, the contact with other artists?" Vicki asked.

She's too direct, Fred thought. Too ready to fix people, to plot their position. He wished she wouldn't pry, but he knew Vicki was good at it. If her probing disquieted him, others seemed unaware of what she was about.

Mathews returned bearing a tray of iced drinks and set it down on a little table in front of them.

"Willy should be back tomorrow," he said, easing into a rocker. "He's probably fixing things right now." He talked on about his plans for the hotel.

"How does this arrangement actually work?" Vicki asked. "Can an American actually own property or is it some sort of lease?"

Mathews was vague. He was counting on Willy Jones doing all the necessary legwork. He waved his hand. "These countries are all alike. Knowing the right people is what matters. Influence."

They sat in the tropical night, he regaling them about his adventures, and needing only the hint of a query from Vicki or Fred to continue. Fortunes made and lost, narrow escapes as a military man in exotic places, a plane crash in which a best friend had been killed, and intimations of closeness with the celebrated. Later he got back to the story of his dream of an island, the decision to give everything up and to retire to this place with his new wife.

"We just put everything in the camper and headed south," he said. "Took our time. Mazatlan, Acapulco, Guatemala, and on down. No big hurry. And then we found this place and learned that Willy wants to sell it."

A stronger breeze fluttered the palm thatch.

"We'll paint everything and get all the screens repaired," said Peggy.

"What about simply buying shares in it?" Fred wondered. "We'd get one month a year here *gratis*. Think of it as just an investment."

"Go to sleep," Vicki murmured, rolling away from Fred. The movement upset his position in the sagging bed and he reached out and cupped her shoulder. She turned over on her back.

"That Mathews," she said. "He's something. A new wife like her, an artist used to life in a city? Expecting her to survive here, isolated like this? He's crazy . . . but she's a wary one. She knows what it's going to be like."

"Where's your romance?"

Vicki sat up. In the cool light of the late rising moon her skin was pale and luminescent.

"He's naïve, and a failure. The way he told you about selling shares in this place—he doesn't know the first thing about it. It's all talk. He couldn't make it in the real world. And he's going to fail here, too."

"You're hard," Fred said. "In a way, I kind of like him. I know what he is, and yet he's not really bad. He's got guts coming down here to this place. I know he's running, but I even admire him for that."

"Go to sleep."

Fred lay on his back looking up at the dark. Why did Mathews remind him of certain boyhood friends? Faces long forgotten came back to him, fellows he had known now and then, all mixtures of doubt and fascination for him. They were usually heartily disliked or distrusted by some of his other friends, or by his mother, but for him they possessed some glittering feature, so that, like a moth to a candle, he was persistently drawn into their influence. One was a tough little ninth grader named Jerry Minck, who worked in a riding stable, shoveling manure and helping with the horses. He was a bully, and Fred had always sensed that Jerry might turn on him at any time, but the attraction was there. He admired the other's rough talk and cocky swagger. Another was Ben Tarsh, roller of tennis courts and handy man at a resort where Fred worked as a waiter the summer after high school. The other waiters, boys of seventeen or so, enjoyed Ben's lurid stories, too, but they were quick to see through him. "Bull-shit," they told Fred, who was held by Ben's assured manner and his apparent knowledge of the world.

Fred chuckled out loud and looked over to see if Vicki was asleep. Ben Tarsh . . . what a guy. And Mathews . . . he was another one.

It was very quiet. The crickets had stopped their music. Up above, in the vague patterns of the roof's shaggy thatch, he lost his way and closed his eyes to enter a dream of Mathews, pebbles on the beach, and blue-green water.

Fred was awakened by noises that overrode the raucous early morning exuberance of the birds. In the palms overhead there were sounds of disturbed leaves and a coming and going of beating wings, but in the last rich moments of sleep there were voices of people talking and a new presence which had not been known before. He opened his eyes. The sun was well up and the room flooded with bright light. Vicki was dressed and standing at the screen door looking out at the beach.

"There's a big yacht coming in," she said.

It was already warm and he threw off the limp sheet.

"What time is it?" he asked.

"Only seven-thirty."

Fred looked at his arm. The red streak was gone and he felt no more tenderness. A tiny scab showed where the scorpion had struck.

He washed, put on a bathing suit and sunglasses, and they walked down to the beach together. In the tranquil light of early morning the yacht's graceful white and mahogany features put to shame the squat little hotel boats anchored just off the beach.

Mathews and Peggy were standing ankle deep in the water.

"Willy's back with some of his friends from the capital," Peggy said in answer to Fred's unspoken question, and they all watched the people disembarking.

"The Gomez brothers," Mathews went on. "The biggest department store is Villa Gomez, and they own liquor stores and a taxi company. One of them has a brother-in-law who was vice-president of the country several years ago."

The men came ashore. Willy Jones was tall, broad-shouldered and ruddy. He greeted them warmly in a loud rough voice and winked at Peggy and Vicki. He seemed in a hurry, but gave Mathews a clap on the back.

Manfredo and José Martin Gomez did not resemble one another at all. Short and muscular, Manfredo had the presence and self-assurance of a man used to holding power over others. José Martin was tall and gaunt with the look of an intellectual. They were introduced briefly.

Willy asked Mathews a question or two about things at the hotel and then said, "I'm taking Manfredo and José Martin up to my place. We'll come down for lunch. And, say, there's a party of six going to be here just to eat and do some swimming. They're about twenty minutes behind us."

"We'll get six extra places set," said Mathews.

Willy and the Gomez brothers began walking up the hill. After a moment, Willy turned and called to Fred.

"Doctor! Manfredo and José Martin are going back to the mainland at four o'clock. They can take you and your wife on their boat. Your train doesn't leave until seven. You'll have lots of time to spare."

Vicki gave Fred an exited smile.

"Let's go on their boat. That's only an hour later than Carlos was going to take us."

"Fine, thanks very much," Fred called out. "We'd like to do that,"

"What do you think they want?" Peggy asked Mathews.

"They probably have some business interests together," he said. "You know—wheeling and dealing."

"When do you expect to know all the final details on the sale of the hotel?" Fred asked.

"It should be very soon," Mathews said. "And if you decide you want to come in on it just let me know and I'll send you the stuff. We'd be glad to have you."

Lunch was noisy and hectic, but Lupe showed up and platters of fish, salad, tortillas, cheese and fruit made their appearance at the long, crowded table. The six new guests, who had come for a day's outing to *Isla Soleada*, were locals from the port on the other side of the gulf. They were in high spirits and spoke only Spanish, although one of the women made a friendly attempt to explain things to Vicki.

Mathews and Peggy seemed energized by the presence of more people and the chatter and general merriment that created a new mood in the hotel. They bustled about, even smiling at Lupe, and showed a new eagerness to accept the responsibilities that would soon fall completely on them.

Willy Jones was genial and even effusive, but when Fred tried to engage him in conversation about the hotel and his plans for the future he evaded the issue and hinted that he didn't have time to go into it. "I'm glad you and your wife have enjoyed yourselves," he said. "When you go back to Minnesota, please tell your friends."

There was never a time to talk privately with Willy.

"Disappointed?" Fred ventured.

"It was fun to think about," Vicki shook her head. "But I have to admit I can't really see us here on a permanent basis."

"Good . . . I didn't want you to be disappointed."

"And you?" she asked.

"Maybe next year."

"Or maybe never?"

"This will sound strange, but Minneapolis seems attractive right now," said Fred.

"I was thinking the same thing."

"Do you think we're beginning to physically resemble each other?"

"No, only dog owners have that problem."

A few minutes after four o'clock the explosive start-up coughs of the yacht's engines modulated into well-mannered purring as it moved elegantly into the gulf like a water-borne monarch. Mathews and Peggy were waving, Willy was swinging the little boy by the arms, and Lupe was standing under a palm tree looking out at the departure. Hotels are sad places, Fred thought. People are always leaving. The boat picked up speed and he watched the figures recede until they dissolved in the trailing blue smoke and the far off haze.

Vicki and Fred settled themselves in the comfort of the yacht. They had gotten under way later than expected. The sun was sinking and the expanse of sky over the gulf was strewn with fields of high clouds touched with lilac.

The operation of the yacht was in the hands of a grizzled old man who sang to himself as he stood at the helm. Manfredo and José Martin sat with the Heaths on the open deck. They had hardly seen the brothers during the day. Willy had taken them on a walk around the island, but Fred had caught glimpses of them peering into buildings and studying the water tank at the top of the hill.

"How did you like your stay at the hotel, *Señora*?" Manfredo Gomez asked. He was digging into an ice chest and emerged with four bottles of cold beer.

"Oh," said Vicki. "It's a peaceful spot—although I usually prefer a more active place. I suppose the island might lose some of its appeal if they spruced it up, but I would rather have a little more comfort."

She ended by looking at Fred, as if to establish her point of view, to gain, by some slight disagreement, an independent position. Manfredo Gomez attended carefully to her comments as he pried the caps from the beer bottles. José Martin had been silent, but his deep-set eyes moved back and forth between the others. Then he bent toward Vicki and his face brightened.

"*Señora*, what would you do to improve the hotel?" he asked.

"Well, you know, paint and clean things up a bit. Have a bowl of fruit out on the table in the bar. Small items like that can make a big difference. And I think the food could be improved. And there should be music. Spanish music. Not loud, but maybe guitars and quiet singing."

"Of course," said José Martin.

"Do you come to the island often?" Fred asked.

"I'm going to be coming more often. My brother and I are taking over the hotel from *Señor* Jones."

Fred had a vision of Mathews waving from the shore.

José Martin went on. "We're going to build a better resort, put in a pool, some nice cabanas."

"What about Mathews?" Fred asked.

"Mathews? Who is Mathews? Oh, I see. No. Mathews—he is out."

The sky to the east was darkening. Only the faintest copper reflection touched the clouds over the mainland and in the little houses along the shore lights were shining through open doors and windows.

JUST THE TICKET

UNSPEAKING AND SELF-ABSORBED, ISAAC, Laura, and Jack sat in the living room with only the rhythmic creaking of Isaac's rocker and the turning of Laura's pages to break the silence. Isaac had put his own book, poems of D.H.Lawrence, face down across his knees, and lulled by the to and fro motion of his chair he stared into the embers of the fire.

He wondered why George hadn't been around for at least four or five days. It was strange because George had become such a very large part of their lives in these last months. Glancing over at Laura, his niece—who seemed these days more like a younger sister to him—he thought she looked disappointed. With her palsy she'd never before had a steady beau, and now it bothered him that they might have rushed George and forced too much of their peculiar hospitality on him.

And they were indeed a peculiar family. George might be having second thoughts.

Once, theirs had been a warm and noisy household, but that had ended with the war and everything that followed—Grandma's death, Isaac's own shell shock, and Jack's divorce.

A peculiar family—no question about it.

Grandma had raised the three of them together—Jack and Laura, who were the children of her deceased eldest daughter, and Isaac, the lone child of her own middle age. If, when they were all kids, Jack had chafed at Isaac being called *uncle,* he quickly learned that it was just one more oddity in the family. If someone was four years younger than you, he could still be your uncle.

No, things had never gotten back to the way they'd been, and that was why George had seemed just the ticket, just the right touch to set them all on a new course. Young, bright, and full of life, he was open and accepting, maybe even charmed by their eccentricities.

On the other hand Isaac worried that George might be pulling away. There was a quality of restraint in George, a limit of privacy beyond which one had better not trespass. Yet, was it too far-fetched to say that George was almost Laura's fiancé? They were together most of the time and there were nights when he stayed late with her, long after Isaac and Jack had gone to bed.

So, why hadn't George called, if only to keep her from worrying? Then there wouldn't have been this silent gloom that filled the house.

George had come into their lives through the ad, and Isaac remembered so clearly the simple, bald words:

> *MEDICAL STUDENT in need of funds to complete*
> *training. Will ensure a premium return on investment.*
> *BOX HM 839, Wall Street Journal.*

A full year had passed since then. In the beginning, suspicion had held Isaac back. The whole idea had been Jack's. Laura, though she thought answering the ad rather silly, had gone along with it in a spirit of adventure. It was also true that Isaac had been just as eager as Jack and Laura for a breath of fresh air. They had become such an odd, cloistral family since the war.

Grandma had died just before VJ Day. Then, when Jack came home from the Pacific, he discovered how Marilyn had been sleeping around and had spent all his service pay on booze and clothes. Bitter and angry, Jack had thrown himself into his business, shutting everything else out of his life.

There they were, the three of them, hurt and peculiar, living together, and staying on where they had grown up in the brick house in Queens with its stoop in front and the alley in back.

How they had all needed something fresh! It was hard to say exactly how George's advent had changed things except that there was more to do now, more to talk about, and of course more to anticipate. Laura, who wore a leg brace, was happy, and Isaac, who had always been especially fond of his niece, had never felt more affection for her.

He hadn't had a relapse or even nightmares about the war in all the time since George had been around. Maybe George was his talisman, too, or maybe it was just seeing Laura so bright and tender looking. Isaac tried to think of other things, but he couldn't keep from being anxious about George not showing up for . . . how long was it? Five days?

He got up from the rocker and held back the curtain to look out into the street. A few cars were parked there and the lampposts rose up like gaunt specters in the cold mist.

> *". . . and our soul cowers naked in the dark rain*
> *over the flood, cowering in the last branches of the tree*
> *of our life . . ."*

He knew that Lawrence might not be the best poet for him to be reading, and involuntarily he murmured into the window "George hasn't been around."

Little vapor prints of his breath expanded on the glass.

Jack stretched at the table where he had been at work on his business accounts, pushed back his chair, and went over to the fireplace.

"Don't worry about George, uncle," said Jack, laughing and poking at the ashes. "You could take a lesson in energy from him. He's on surgery. He's working his tail off."

Laura slammed her book shut and changed her position on the couch. "You know he's never *on* five days in a row," she said. Her palsy was only in her legs and, though fairly mild, she had to use her shoulders and arms a lot when she wanted to move around.

"I don't get it," she said. "I called the hospital. They say he was on two nights ago, but not since." She looked from one to the other with her deep-set brown eyes.

"Ah, don't worry," said Jack. He sat down with his papers again. "He'll be around. I've got great faith in him, and besides, I haven't ever made any foolish investments."

"Don't say that," Laura began, but she broke it off and opened her book again.

Isaac went into the kitchen and dialed George's apartment in Brooklyn. It rang four, six, eight, ten times. He thought about the unapproachable aspect of George, his slightly mystifying quality. Where the hell was he? Didn't he ever go home to his place?

"I'll start dinner," he called, hanging up. He took things out of the refrigerator and set them on the counter. Laura came in looking glum and they were silent as they moved about washing potatoes, scraping carrots, and setting things to boil and cook.

Isaac sometimes had to be taken to the VA hospital out at Northport, but most days he was clear-eyed and sane. There had been times when he would begin saying things in a disconnected way and then Jack and Laura would watch him carefully for more signs of another relapse.

After being drafted, Isaac's unit was sent to London to await deployment into France in mid-June 1944. He missed the initial Normandy invasion by a week and would have been in the second wave of troops to land there, but the war came to him in London right when the Germans began attacking the city with V-1 buzz bombs. The noise and confusion were too much for him and it made him crazy.

He ended up running around screaming his head off, and when the MPs tried to restrain him he nearly bit off one's thumb. They clobbered his head with nightsticks and it was never very clear whether his troubles stemmed from that beating or whether they were completely psychiatric. Jack, who had seen plenty of combat in the Pacific with the Navy, had his own theory that Isaac was basically lazy. He had a hunch that the intermittent rest periods at the VA were just that and nothing more.

"This world is for go-getters," he would say. "Books are fine. I read books, too, but you've got to step up to life. You can't expect anything good to happen if you moon around."

It was true that Jack read books, but his reading was unique in that he was on the way through the Britannica and had gotten up to "H." Isaac did have a now-and-then job as a reporter on the *Long Island Star Journal,* and that enabled him to pay his share of the living expenses, but his real love was poetry. He'd never shown his seventeen poems to anyone, including Jack and Laura, although both knew about them. Once he had mentioned to Jack that the young Walt Whitman had also worked as a journalist on Long Island papers. Jack ignored this. He had never been able to take it seriously. The two of them were so different.

Jack wasn't fair. Isaac felt that even for Jack business was a dead end, and that despite his own emotional instability he at least had hopes for a real future—a sense of possibility. But at other times he had doubts, too. He was ashamed of what had happened to him in London because Jack had been through just as much. Jack was bitter over Marilyn, but he had certainly carved himself a niche and wasn't drifting, as Isaac felt he was doing.

What value do I have for the world? Isaac asked himself. I smoke too much, and I've put on weight. I'm even in awe of George's medical career.

In the beginning, when they had first seen the ad, Isaac had held back from the whole thing because it was such a dare and so strange. Jack didn't read the Wall Street Journal much, but subscribed to it because he said it made him feel like a real businessman. When he came across the ad he said he liked its honesty and that only an eager, young go-getter would have the guts to put in an ad like that. He said it meant George was a good man. Anyway, Isaac thought, it was Jack's money. And unquestionably, Jack did all right with his mail order gimmicks and his little ads on the back covers of comic books. From his tiny office down in the basement he cleared nine thousand a year.

The arrangement was very simple. George had finished two years of medical school and needed eight hundred dollars. Since he was going to join the Army Medical Corps after graduation he would be able to pay it back easily with some sort of interest. They all liked him right from the start and after a while they forgot about the crazy way it had started. Despite the *chutzpah* of the ad George had this quiet air about him, this portion of reserve. He never said much about his family who lived somewhere back in Washington or Idaho. And there was another thing—he wasn't Jewish.

George's last name was Blum and they had never imagined that he wasn't Jewish. The subject had never come up. He seemed Jewish to them, and that was good enough.

Then one day, several months after Jack had loaned him the money, George said, "You know, before I came to New York I never met any Jews."

That stopped the conversation, but a short history lesson from Jack and Isaac, and some unsophisticated but friendly responses from George seemed to satisfy everybody, at least for the time being.

Isaac brought it up a few times to Jack and Laura when George wasn't around, but Jack got irritated and told Isaac he didn't want to hear any more about it.

"I say the hell with being Jewish and the hell with his family," he snapped. "Marilyn was Jewish, and look what a tramp she turned out to be."

Isaac listened and Laura listened, but neither of them wanted to interrupt him.

"It makes no difference," Jack went on. "All we need to know is that Laura likes him and he likes Laura. He's a hard working guy and he'll do well. That's all."

There was no doubt George liked Laura. He seemed attracted to her right from the start and Laura had never let her palsy hold her back. She drove a car, she took courses at Queens College, and she had plans to become a social worker. Once, a boy with palsy, a classmate at the special school she'd attended, had been in love with her, but she had seen him only as a friend. With George it was different. Whatever he saw in her responded and grew with his attentions. She seemed to bloom before their eyes. She even seemed lighter on her feet and less clumsy. It wasn't that George had declared himself. There was nothing official yet. He took her to the movies and out driving. But, what Isaac noted most was that when the four of them were together, George always seemed to find a way to look at Laura, to seek her approval for what he said. If he were talking to Jack or to Isaac he always managed to include Laura in a way that said it was really she to whom he spoke.

But he never touched her. Isaac had never seen George hold her hand except to assist her into the car or to hold a chair for her. If it was love, they were hiding the evidence. But Isaac had no doubt that the more demonstrative moments were saved for late in the evening or the early hours when he and Jack were asleep. One morning at seven he had come down in his robe and was amazed to see George sitting on the couch.

"It was too late to go home," he explained, rubbing his face.

They sat down and ate quietly. Isaac had put a new LP with Haydn string quartets on the phonograph, and the music seemed to soothe everyone.

Jack pointed to his watch. "Well, it's almost eight o'clock," he said. Laura nodded, but didn't say anything.

Jack put out his hand and patted her forearm. "I'm sure he's okay."

He couldn't see her face because she was facing away, but when she turned he could see the tears.

"Oh, don't," he said gently. "Don't get upset."

"Five days?" She faced him and shook her head. "Something's happened."

He watched her, not knowing what to say or do, but then she pushed away from the table, pulled herself up, and limped down to her room.

Isaac let his fork drop on the plate and clenched his fists. "Oh, God," he said. "We should do something."

"Ah, come on," Jack replied. "Leave it alone. We can't control everything."

"What if he needs us?"

Jack considered this but shook his head.

"You mean . . . illness? What?"

"I don't know."

They didn't say anything for a while. Isaac started clearing the table. In a few minutes Jack could hear the water running in the kitchen and the sounds of dishes and pots being washed.

He went in and grabbed a towel to dry. They finished up without speaking, but Laura's door opened and she came out. She had her coat on.

"I want to go there," she said. "I want to make sure."

A white half-moon hung in the chill autumn sky. Jack backed the Olds out, and they headed for the Interborough, barely speaking as they approached Brooklyn.

Jack drove carefully. Taxis passed them, but otherwise very few cars were on the road.

George had the front apartment in a two-family house near Kings County Hospital. When they pulled up along the curb the place looked dark, but Laura said, "No, there's light flickering in the window."

They went up the five steps to the little porch. Someone was talking inside, but it stopped when they rang the bell.

They heard a step. The knob turned and George's silhouette filled the doorway with candlelight behind.

"Oh, hi," he said, taking in the three standing before him on the stoop. "What . . .?"

He moved a bit, directed a quick glance over his shoulder, and then faced them again with a broad smile. "Well . . ."

Laura was the first to see.

"Oh," she blurted.

Everything was there before them: the candles on the little table, dishes of spaghetti and glasses of dark wine carefully placed on the red and white checkered cloth. And the girl—a slender girl with long hair easing up out of her chair, and coming forward to stand behind George. She smiled—gentle, and tentative, and apologetic.

"We've been worried about you," Isaac said.

But Laura had turned away. "No," she murmured. "No."

George looked stricken, but still managed to flash a recurring nervous smile.

"Sorry, I . ., this is Mary . ., my fiancé . . ."

Laura was beginning to navigate back down the steps. Jack grabbed her arm.

"Sorry," George said again.

Isaac nodded. "Yeah," he said. "Yeah, we get it."

Then he turned and followed his niece and nephew down.

"We get it."

She cried softly, saying little bits of phrases between her sobs as they drove home.

"How could he? I feel so dirty."

Her humiliation was only a part of their embarrassment. There was also the feeling, and Isaac sensed that Laura shared it, that they had all looked in on a scene that was too intimate for anyone but those other two. Even if George was a bastard, and the girl a floozy, they'd seen and disturbed a private thing. It seemed wrong, and somehow unforgiveable.

For a moment Jack wanted to express that to Laura, but he couldn't. It was impossible. She was so sad and exhausted. As he drove along the darkened parkway, the thought kept coming back, and it bothered him more than the obvious betrayal. He knew that the image of their intrusion would haunt him forever—cornering them there like two small animals that had no chance of fighting back.

He kept shaking his head.

No one spoke for the rest of the trip home.

Loss

A NEWSPAPER LIES AT MY feet. On page twelve there's an account of the revolution in the Republic. A perversely incomplete, not to mention fundamentally false account, but the anger I feel and my helplessness to do anything about it won't keep me from telling the story as I have lived it.

While my exhausted wife sleeps, I write at this desk in our Miami hotel room eight floors above the sparkling blue-green sea.

I've heard that those glittering bits of light on the water are photons that began the first part of their journey from the sun's core over a thousand years ago. Then, inexorably, they left the sun's surface to reach the earth, over ninety million miles away, in just eight minutes.

Our journey across the same sea took days, but there is much more to tell.

I have to put aside anger.

Perhaps I will recapture the sweetness of my homeland and the love I still hold for it.

1

On the narrow coastal plain that skirts the base of high mountains the nights remain hot until long after the sun goes down. Men relish the late hours when they may take their ease, sipping drinks, talking, and feeling the balmy fragrant air that begins, finally, to hint of coolness on the skin. For with all its lush beauty the land is harsh and treacherous, and the men who daily wrest a living from it need a time to recover. At night the brutal climate and the ceaseless struggle are softened for those few hours, and the graces of rest and conversation work small soothing miracles.

On such a night I sat with my friend, Rafael Salazar, on the high porch of his farmhouse. As the representative of the Pope in the Republic, Salazar is a man of considerable prestige and dignity, but his official duties are few and he spends most days cloistered at his ancestral farm engaged in writing a history of the Church in the Spanish colonial period. Salazar is a man of epicurean tastes and culture and except for the matter of his birth he has often seemed to me out of place in our sultry and impoverished Republic. But, he has the capacity to take each day as it comes to him, and he has told me that at the back of his mind there is a secure feeling that his exile in the tropical land of our birth has finite bounds. Sometime, perhaps when his book is finished, Rome will again send him out into the world he cherishes most, where men and women of charm and wit live in great metropolitan cities surrounded by art and graciousness. Meanwhile, he has his work, and there is not a better place for it than Puerto Cangrejo where the daily life of people has barely changed since colonial days. He pores over long ecclesiastical tracts in Latin and accounts of local parishes written in the Spanish of the sixteenth century. With loving care he transforms these and, as he writes, the colors of the land, the brooding green of the jungle and the brilliant reds and yellows of birds and flowers, the oppressive heat, the rutted roads, the dark-skinned people with their rags and long knives . . . all these find their way into his writing and infuse it, vivid and sensual. Rafael Salazar, fat and serene, is the last of his line, but with a secret discomfiture in his quiet life when his thoughts turn to the rich turbulent blood of his Conquistador ancestors.

For long moments we two sat quietly, saying nothing. There were just the small incessant sounds of the tropical night coming through the wire screen and filling the air between us—the chirruping of myriad insects, and the shrill broken cries of birds and small animals. Only a dim light came from the parlor behind us, and our features were in shadow as we faced out across the grass to the jungle-covered mountains beyond.

"Why can't you bend a little, Antonio?" Salazar asked me.

It was too dark for each to see what lay on the surface of the other's face, but we were old friends, and I knew he was aware of the vexation I felt after that remark. His words certainly annoyed me, and for an instant I almost stood up to leave, but I wanted the understanding of my friend.

"Listen to me," I said finally. "I am obstinate, but obstinate because I am right. I'm disappointed that you turn on me. You, of all people—a blueblood."

My reaction was no mystery to my host. He knew the Nasrif family's history all too well, and I am, or I was on that night, its leader. Nasrif—a Christian Arab family that fled the Ottoman Empire and emigrated to the Republic in 1890. *Turcos*, the locals call us. My father built up our large mercantile empire, but I increased and solidified the holdings, and it is no boast to say that I was the wealthiest and most important businessman in Puerto Cangrejo. It is simply a fact.

Salazar looked down into his glass of Scotch. In the dark his bulk was what one noticed—the thick hair brushed back on the big jowled head, the heavy shoulders sloping down to the barrel of his body.

"Forget my heredity, *amigo*," he said. "This is a matter of common sense."

"No, Rafael. Vargas-Macayo is a troublemaker. His demands are stupid and unworkable. I am only one landowner. I don't make policy for the whole Republic."

"Others will follow your lead, Antonio."

I shifted in my chair to face him. "He's a fool. All that blather about how the Nasrif family interests are tied to the American fruit company. Of course we're tied together. I sell them hardware when they need it."

"You need to be more open-minded, Antonio. He may irritate you, but he's no fool. The students worship him. He's a real leader, a man with appeal."

"Fine," I said, not knowing how to respond. I stood and began pacing back and forth along the porch. I am tall and dark, and a random thought came to me that the white material of my loose cotton shirt must have seemed to float disembodied, like a phosphorescent curtain advancing and retreating in the night.

"You know how it looks, *amigo*," said Salazar. "You're pals with Jenkins and the other *gringos*."

"For Christ's sake, Rafael. If it weren't for an American fruit company where do you think we'd be around here? Who would run things without the *gringos*? Could Vargas-Macayo, with all of his hot air, manage an operation like that? The engineering, the shipping, the financing? You know what the trouble is as well as I do. These people are lazy, Rafael. It's in their blood. They're like animals. Given the choice, most of them would prefer lying around drunk. They're lucky there's work for them."

"They are poor people, Antonio. The poor have never had much choice."

I knew I had uttered, out of anger and frustration, something clumsy, harsh and crude, but I was talking to a close friend and I hoped he could understand.

"What about my own father?" I argued. "Didn't he come here poor? He worked hard for what he got, and I'll be damned if I'll give it away to that bastard and his crowd."

"No one is asking you to give anything away. If it were that radical I would agree with you."

"Profit-sharing, a gradual reapportionment of land? What difference does it make what name you give to it? It comes to the same thing. Take it from us, and give it to them."

My words reverberated painfully, like the discord of a badly played instrument.

"Sometimes," I began again. "Sometimes I wish . . . Ah, to hell with it."

"What do you wish?"

"Nothing."

I looked out into the night, twirling the ice cubes in my glass and tears welled up in my eyes as I thought about what I wanted to tell my friend. There was no one else I could talk to in this way.

"Rafael . . ."

"Go on."

"It sounds crazy. I would like to give it all up. Get out of this place. It's a terrible thing to admit, but I hate this town, the Republic, the whole thing."

"Where would you go?"

"I don't know. The States. Europe."

"How could you? You have enormous responsibilities here."

"That's the point. I could do without them. Sell the farm, the businesses."

"But no one could run them. You know that."

"No . . . certainly not José Miguel."

"You're disappointed in your son?"

"That's not news to you."

Salazar reached out and touched my forearm. "Look, *amigo*, I love you. We are kindred spirits, but everyone has duties particular to him. Call them God-given, if you will. Wait—let me finish. Yours are different from mine. I am alone, a scholar, a futile cleric. You have in your hands the lives and welfare of many people. You were born to these responsibilities just as I have my duties."

"But I don't need this power. I can go away."

"Ah . . . it's an illusion. We all have that dream." He reached forward and poured the last drops of Scotch into my glass. "It's empty," he said, rising from his chair, and shuffled across the porch into the house.

The sky was black. No stars. Distant low rumbling threatened a storm. I got up and went into the parlor. It was a large cluttered room with straw mats on the floor. Against one wall stood tall bookcases, but books of all sorts, old leather bound folios together with paperback novels, had outgrown the bounds of the shelves and lay on the floor in irregular piles. On the end wall hung a group of paintings, again a mixture. Old colonial portraits of Saints; armor-clad Spanish noblemen; modern primitive watercolors of local scenes. A long mahogany table stood before the wall and on it I saw the typewriter and pages of manuscript, the latest phase in my friend's unusual career.

Beyond, in the kitchen, I could hear Salazar opening the refrigerator.

Years before, his teachers had known with some embarrassment that the young student's piety was only barely adequate. He had an impish way of questioning that put them off, but they swallowed their chagrin when they realized his brilliance. He astounded them with a rare genius for rhetoric, history, and politics, and they decided that the Republic was too confined a sphere for such talents. I remember clearly the day when Rafael Salazar, wearing a black suit and seminarian's hat, walked in his squat way down the wharf to board one of the fruit ships. He was beginning the long journey that ended finally at Rome where he was to be groomed for a career in Catholic diplomacy. Eventually he had become the youngest Papal Nuncio ever to serve in several different countries, and he achieved moderate fame and power within the hierarchy.

Not quite enough, however. At the age of forty-four he was sent back to the country of our birth. Notwithstanding, he seemed content with this, and I, especially, welcomed his return. In all of Puerto Cangrejo there was no one who knew the world as Rafael Salazar had known it, and sometimes I felt that by talking to my friend, I, Antonio Nasrif, was escaping the narrow life of our steamy port on the sea. I saw a vision of the continents beyond; of poetry and art; the historic cities of Europe; and the great world of ideas and philosophy. Rafael was easy and discursive about what his life in Europe and in South America had been and the grand images nourished my soul. For a long time I had the feeling that perhaps I had been meant for another sort of life. Maybe it had been only a chance of birth that had made of me a man of commerce.

When Salazar emerged from the kitchen he placed an ice bucket and another bottle of Scotch on the table.

"I just want to say one more thing about that business," he said to me. "Then we can go on to something else, which is even more important. If you can bring yourself to do it, that is. Just let Vargas-Macayo know in some small way that you respect him as a man, and that you give consideration to what he says. That's all. You needn't agree to anything. Just let him know that you are listening. That will be a beginning."

"A beginning of the end for us."

"All right. That's enough. Now . . . what is this I hear about José Miguel?"

A child comes into the world fresh and malleable, and young parents are inexperienced and ignorant. Being shaped by their own particular histories, they nurture or ruin these tender beings. Sometimes they do both.

Rafael Salazar said I was disappointed in my son, and I don't deny it. I nurtured, but also contributed to ruining José Miguel. It was a gradual thing—not one bad step, not one disaster, but a general ambience, a tenor, a steady neglect of which I was oblivious or even determined to ignore.

At any rate, my colossal indifference is part of the background. I accept it. José Miguel is as much a part of this story as I am.

2

In the dusty arena the cock's eyes glittered like bits of yellow glass, and its neat, feathered head made small nervous pivots. It was over-stimulated by the shouting and the proximity of other birds.

José Miguel Nasrif, its owner, relaxed the cord that held it by the leg and the cock darted forward seeking an opponent. Its beak jerked from side to side and it hopped into the air a few inches. José Miguel drew it back and covered its head with a small leather hood.

"He's a little light, kid," Nacho, the sailor, said to José Miguel. "But he's a spunky bugger."

"Spunky my ass," said Monkey-Killer. "He'll wilt. These shrimp birds never last."

Monkey-Killer was a short, crooked old man with big hair-filled nostrils that widened when he got excited. He caught monkeys in the mountains, ate their meat, and sold the pelts to the gift shop. But, he was a regular at the cockfights and although he would rarely place a bet, he was always in the arena feeling the birds, appraising them, and giving opinions.

"Three-to-one that half-blind stalwart will cut him to shreds," he said, pointing across the ring to a cock being taken from its cage by a farmer in white pajamas. The farmer, who was from Remedios, was a broad-backed mixed breed of Indian and Negro with a dark, hostile face. His red bird was scruffy and scarred, and had a cloudy eye.

"Stick to monkeys, old man," said Nacho, clapping Monkey-Killer on the back. There was laughter in the arena and a bottle was being passed back and forth by the men who leaned against the blood spattered plaster wall of the inner ring. More people were gathering in the stands. Ortiz, the pharmacist, was there in his tan jacket and black tie. He was the only man in town who ever wore a tie. Montoya, the surgeon, wiped a seat with his white handkerchief, and then settled back with a long cigar. Nacho moved around the ring arranging bets.

"Hello, there, Consul," he yelled at Lucchese, the movie theatre owner, who sat in the top row fanning himself with a newspaper.

"Looking for a little action, Consul?"

Lucchese had a title because he was the official representative of Italy in the port, but in the twenty-five years he had lived in Puerto Cangrejo he had never had to perform officially more than once or twice a year. It was usually to stand up before the Police Court in cases where Italian sailors had taken their lovemaking a little too seriously and had been beaten up by pimps.

"I'll go with José Miguel's bird," the Consul called down to Nacho.

Other cock owners stood in the ring, feeling the birds and estimating their weights. The air under the tin roof was dense, hot, and expectant. Flies circled slowly. José Miguel wiped sweat from his forehead and held his little fighter. It was an important moment. He had bought it for one hundred pesos in the capital and had seen it fight well against smaller birds, but here in Puerto Cangrejo where the rules were looser his bird would be pitted against a wider variety of competitors. He was uneasy about the farmer from Remedios. He sensed that behind the peasant's impassivity was a proud and shrewd man who would only put up a proven cock. Sometimes a poor looking bird turned out to be a mean fighter and his scarred ugliness the badge of a long stubborn career.

"These two," said Nacho to the crowd. He pointed to José Miguel and then across at the farmer in white pajamas. There was laughter among the spectators. José Miguel crouched with his bird and took a small black box from his shirt pocket The thin knives lay inside on a piece of denim, honed to the sharpness of diminutive razors. He lifted them out gingerly and fastened them, spur-like, to the bird's legs. The farmer was crouched down opposite, busy with his own scruffy bird. José Miguel felt a change of mood. He had a sudden inkling that his own bird would beat the tired old beggar bird from Remedios. For a moment the farmer's eyes met his own—fierce, dark, and unnerving. Brooding, restrained animosity.

Now they were ready. They held the two birds at the edge of the circle. The hoods were removed, and at a signal from Nacho they set them free. The birds darted at each other. The action was quick and furious. A shout of amazement went up from the crowd as the scruffy red wheeled and slashed at José Miguel's bird. Blood oozed from the smaller bird's chest. Frenzied, it turned about, trying to find a target for its own knives, but it weakened and fell under another attack from the scarred battler. Finally, it dropped and José Miguel ran out to revive it. He blew air into its beak and in a moment the little body stirred in his hands. It began struggling to get free and José Miguel set it back down in the dust. In a flash it was at the other bird, but wobbling and dizzy, and the enemy drove knives deep into its belly. Finally, it fell dead. The bird from Remedios darted to the side and began running around the arena.

José Miguel stepped out to pick up his bird, and as he did the victorious bird suddenly flew at him. José Miguel hit out with his hand to protect himself. He felt the impact of his palm against the warm feathered creature, and then the lancinating sensation of the bird's knives ripping into his palm.

In the next instant he was aware of a broad body in white pajamas that flew at him, knocking him to the ground. A heavy weight lay on him, pushing his head into the dirt of the floor and suddenly everyone was shouting, but as if from far away. He could taste the earth and squirmed under the terrible pressure on the bones of his neck. And then, just as quickly, they had pulled the farmer off him and José Miguel looked down at his hand spurting bright red blood. Nacho was wrapping a rag around it.

Monkey-Killer and three other men restrained the farmer, but he was struggling furiously and screaming.

"Fucking *turco*! Son of a whore!"

3

What was my city—Puerto Cangrejo—lies packed into a short stretch along the coast of the Republic. It is a grid of streets with two-story buildings, tin-roofed, and mostly of white painted wood. Some houses have a portico, and many have a balcony made of decorative ironwork that juts out over the sidewalk—a good viewpoint for children and old women to peer at what goes on below.

Things are mud spattered and rusty. There are dilapidated shaky buses with hoods that won't stay down, the racks on top piled with wooden crates of chickens and the tattered bundles of passengers. In early morning before cockcrow, when the stars are in their last bright moments, old men with pitiful brooms made of twigs sweep along the prior day's accumulated dusty detritus—donkey manure, mango pits, cigar butts, rotten fruit.

There is no order in the profusion of commercial signs crowding the facades of deteriorating store fronts, but what was our family's hardware emporium, *Ferreteria Nasrif,* is a clean looking modern building at one corner of the public square. Beyond it, looking down the broad main street, one has a view to the sea where the wharf stretches far out and loitering men watch the ships taking on bananas.

It is not at all strange that Arab families made their way to Central American lands that were colonized by Spaniards. The rich infusion of Arab blood that fertilized medieval Spain is known to all and must have seemed an assurance of welcome. That was certainly true for my family, and for a long time we did very well in the Republic.

It is a poor country, but anyone can see that life has improved. Despite the anemic and malnourished children whose skin is the color of pale mud, one learns not to stare. If their fathers work for the fruit company, they're paid well—better than by other employers. Still, like everything else, luck has a lot to do with it. There are not enough jobs to go around.

No one can deny that the fruit company has been a great help to the economy, and I, for one, counted among my friends the director and many of the engineers who run things. They were always grateful to our family. We were well connected, we had all the latest equipment, and our business ethic was as American as that of any firm in the States.

The problem with someone like Vargas-Macayo was his resentment of people who are more adept at business and able to accumulate wealth. Things do become unequal, but that is the way of the world, and he had no real answer for it except to rage at his betters. He was paranoid and imagined that the Americans at the fruit company got advice from our family—an oligarchy, he called it—on how to manipulate the local population.

I knew Vargas-Macayo forever. We were boys together, and for a time at the same school, but friendship was impossible. He was a bully, and I was afraid of him. Moreover, he was a Negro, and very black. There was a story that his mother had been one of the whores at Madame Trucha's before her marriage, but one never taunted him about that or about anything else.

When we were ten years old, Vargas-Macayo's family took him away to the capital and I assumed he was gone from my life. It was only years later that he reappeared on the coast as a labor organizer, then a teacher, and, finally, as the dean of the agricultural college. Puerto Cangrejo is so small that it was inevitable we would sometimes run into each other, but we had nothing in common and even less to discuss. Broad shouldered and of medium height, he wore a loose fitting *guayabera*, and, with the iron-rimmed spectacles he wore on his round ebony face, he still had more the look of a dockworker than a professor.

I might never have had any more thought about him, until one day I learned from an acquaintance that Vargas-Macayo's daughter had been seen with my son. At first I paid no attention, but soon others began talking, and I finally confronted José Miguel.

"I have nothing to hide," my son told me. "She and I are friends."

"How can that be?"

"I don't know what you mean," he replied.

"It's not appropriate."

"Why? Because she's black?"

"Not at all," I said defensively. "But our positions are quite different."

"Maybe that's not so important any more."

"Don't be stupid."

My son turned away. "Why do you bother me about this? It's my life."

"No, it's more than that. Her father is a communist. He is jealous of anyone who has worked hard and earned a place . . ."

"Yes, yes . . . I know your argument. But you should relax. This is none of your . . ."

I slapped him.

It was the beginning of the most painful estrangement of my life.

4

The apprenticeship in power was easy for me. Even as a boy I learned quickly how to manage people, how to get what I wanted. I was made to feel that, as the son of a powerful man, respect was due me. I grasped how to talk to servants, to men who worked in the store, and to farm hands and cowboys. Everyone deferred to me, and I tried to believe it was because of admiration for my abilities, but I knew otherwise.

I was never shown the warmth, and even love, that the local people had for my father. To them he was Don Marinero—approachable, even in his crafty shrewdness and strength. All kinds of people liked him. Probably even from childhood I knew I was apart from the common folk. The ragged beggars and malaria-ridden women in the streets had little connection to me.

When I came back to the Republic after my years of schooling in the United States everyone said I was a changed young man, but I knew that meant they saw me as cool and more distant than ever. Their disdain hurt, and I felt it unfair, but I didn't dwell on it. I was back in my own country and I had my task—to learn all I could about the running of the family enterprises.

We were not in the government, nor in the Army, but from the hardware store on the square the Nasrif family had extended its influence for many years and in many directions. As a boy I sensed that the iron tools and dusty bins of nails only camouflaged secrets being made daily in the cluttered back office. Men came and talked with my father and then went out to serve the family in mysterious ways. It was only after I came home from those years in the States that I really began to learn the intricate web of relationships that conferred wealth and power on us.

My father had come from Palestine many years before, a Christian fleeing Ottoman oppression, and he was fond of telling us children how it had been.

"I wore rags and a pistol in my belt," he would laugh.

"And why did they call you Don Marinero?"

"Because I came out of the sea."

Many people still knew the story of how he came piloting a tiny dinghy with a tattered sail made from an overcoat. He wore a gold cross on a chain around his neck and carried a Turkish passport, but the details of his voyage remained vague because at that time he barely spoke Spanish. It was known that he had first been in the United States. "*New Orleans*" was stamped on the passport and he had some American dollars, but the mystery lingered of how he had come south across hundreds of miles of open sea. He was short and wiry, with black hair and the thin sensitive features of the Levant, and he displayed an imperturbable poise and a gentle evasiveness that led people to say he had something of the wild animal in him. The customs men, suspicious at first, quickly became his allies after it became clear he had enough money to buy a horse and to rent a room in the flea-ridden Paris Hotel where he lived those first few months. Behind his back they called him *turco,* but they also elevated him to *Don Marinero,* and when my father died he owned the large cattle farm and the only hardware business on the Caribbean side of the Republic.

"There is some power in business," he told me. "But when you compound businesses the web grows and you have great power." Nothing in the town occurred without his knowledge, very little without his permission.

The family was small. He had sent to Palestine for a wife when he felt himself established after years of hard work. Although he'd left behind a way of life that his ancestors practiced for centuries, there remained in him a robust conviction that some of those traditions were to be honored. He could have chosen well from among several Arab families who had come to the new country, but none of them would do. He wanted a wife from over the sea. It seemed more fitting to him, more commanding of respect, and Maria Mahin came from Bethlehem. Dignified, calm, and industrious, she bore him two girls, Angelica and Blanca, and then, two years later, presented him with a male heir when I came into the world.

I was spoiled by my sisters and adored by my parents. One of my earliest memories is of being jolted in a rough wagon drawn by a mule along a palm-lined track. Father, his dark face framed by a straw sombrero, smiled down at me, and I wore the new boots he had given me, shining brown leather that came up the calf, fitting like soft gloves. We were going to a farm to see the cows that Father was about to buy. Later, I stood in the chalky dirt next to the corral, inhaling smells of hay and manure, and trying to talk to the wary, sad-eyed animals, but fearful of their long-horned tossing heads. I was only half aware of voices raised in argument, but I saw the flash of the machete and Father ducking to avoid the blow. Then shouts, a scuffling in the dust, and Father, like a dancer, leaping toward the man and hitting him across the face with the barrel of his pistol. The man ran off and the others stood back. None of the men had shoes—not even a tall Negro who wore a pair of broken spurs on his scabby feet. I began sobbing and pressed my cheek against the log rail of the corral. Father put the pistol back in his belt and walked over to the man with the spurs. He said a few words and the man nodded. Then we got into the wagon and headed back home.

"Who was that tall man?" I asked.

"His name is Cecil. This was his farm."

"Did you buy the cows?" I asked through my tears.

"Yes," Father said. "And the farm, too."

Some years later my sisters and I drove with Father one Saturday to the farm to pay the men. A cloud of dust whirled up around our new truck as we bumped along the road.

"Mama says the men are crude," I said, looking up at giant trees festooned with lianas.

"They are just men," Father said. "Your mother doesn't like the farm."

The jungle became thick and more oppressive, the road attenuated and squeezed on both sides and from above by leafy walls of dark green. At a shallow ford in the river the road dipped down and the truck splashed across. Listless women with skirts hoisted stood in the muddy water washing clothes. Their children played among the rocks throwing stones at vultures that cawed and strutted in the shadows.

"Tell us about Cecil," I asked. We had heard stories about brawls over women and how Cecil had hidden in the jungle to escape the police. People said he had killed seven men—in self-defense. And there were secrets between him and my father—nights when Cecil appeared at our door and left quietly with a bag of food.

"No one knows the truth about Cecil," Father sighed. "Not even I. The important thing is that he's a good foreman. And remember this: when I bought the farm I paid him a fair price. In fact, I was generous. He will always be loyal."

We turned down a lane between barbed wire fences. When we reached the gate Father blew the horn several times and we waited until a thin boy appeared out of the brush to open it for us. He was about my age and raised his hand to shield his expressionless eyes from the sun as he looked up at the truck. We moved through and he stood holding the gate for us. I waved back at him, but he'd already turned away.

At the corral the men were lounging under the trees. A few women in cotton dresses stood there, some of them holding children, waiting for the money. I went with my sisters to look at the horses tied to a hitch rail. Cecil brought us bottles of lemon soda and we leaned against the rail, sipping and brushing away the flies.

All the men except for Cecil gathered about Don Marinero as he paid them, peeling off paper notes from the big roll he carried. Cecil stood to one side, watching. There was a grievance. One of the men had done some extra work and was asking for more money. Father merely smiled and gave him another note. The man thanked him and backed away. I saw Cecil spit.

"We don't want any more, Papa," said Angelica. She and Blanca held out their half empty bottles, and Father pointed to the children of the men who squatted under a large tree.

"Give it to them," he said.

Four children walked over, took the bottles, and then, laughing and joking, shared the remaining soda. I still held my empty bottle, but a little girl came over to me. She took the bottle from me and placed it in a carton next to the barn.

"You see?" Father smiled at me. "If you give them something to eat, they will work for you."

5

Cecil worked for the Nasrif family even before I was born. At first he was an all-purpose helper, but as foreman of the farm he sold to us, he loomed large. There was watchfulness in him, a powerful, judging kind of regard that made me uneasy. Part of it was his unsmiling silence, part of it his strength. As much as my father trusted him, I feared the man.

Much later, I had one particular brief moment of watching Cecil from a distance, and through all the years that came afterwards I have never forgotten how it justified in me the doubts about him that

I had carried from childhood. Even the smallest details are clear in my mind.

It was only a few months before my father died. The mayor and other important people in Puerto Cangrejo decided to hold a testimonial dinner to honor Don Marinero for his philanthropy.

The air was humid and balmy. This was the big social event of the season. Business leaders and senators had come from the capital to celebrate my father. People were mixing and milling about on the crowded patio of the Caribe Restaurant. Two guitarists played and sang softly in the background. There were extravagant spreads of food and expensive wines. Conviviality was the note of the evening and everyone was talking. No one paid attention to the insouciant grackles that shamelessly hopped up on tables to steal bits of food. A dour cigarette girl in too short a white skirt with red piping wandered about, her face a mix of bashfulness and a look in which one couldn't distinguish boredom from suppressed rage at having to stand there pressing her wooden box of cigarettes and cigars against her rounded stomach.

Finally, one after another, men rose to toast Father's health and to recall a good deed or some human quality of the old man. People drank, clapped their hands, and smiled at one another. I was very proud to be my father's son.

Then I glimpsed Cecil's frowning black face. He stood under the portico with others who listened to the speeches and who wanted to share something of the festive evening. But those were servants and workers, and not expected to participate. The real guests paid no attention to them, but the angry look on Cecil's face upset me, and the fear I felt lingered for weeks.

I am proud that I enlarged the scope of our family's holdings. The hub was *Ferreteria Nasrif* and we also had the farm, but I was quick to see neglected opportunities. The Republic had an undependable system for the transport of goods, so I decided to take advantage of the situation. That was the start of our hugely profitable trucking company. My decision to start a distillery was even more valuable. Within a few years we were making most of the *aguardiente* produced in the Republic, and very soon we were exporting high quality liquors to Europe and the States.

I liked Father's stories about the history of our family, but most of the time I was immersed in my own life. As much as I wanted to emulate his skill in business, my mother, Maria Mahin, had at least an equal part in shaping the person I was to become. She had grown up in a comfortable home in Bethlehem, and had high aspirations for me. Her own father had been a doctor who had trained in Paris. Sensitive and talented, she loved music, theatre, and art. Some saw her as timid and a little frightened of my father, but what others deemed passivity Don Marinero knew was promise. The pauses in her speech when her dark eyes were appraising a listener meant not weakness, but strength. She never accepted events or people at face value, but questioned everything and was able to reach insights that were lost on others. My father knew he had made the right choice. They fell deeply in love, and despite being uprooted from her life in Palestine, my mother adapted quickly to the new country.

Each of my parents had a core of steel. He taught me about competition in the world, and gave me the strength and understanding to do well in the world of business. She instilled in me a desire for the beautiful, and for the life of the mind, but I cannot blame her for making me into a misfit in that steaming tropical backwater where nature overcomes civilization and introspection can become a paralyzing disability. I did that myself.

When I came back from the university most of my time was devoted to commerce. Then, at twenty-two, I met Rosalba Lara. She was slim and pale, and I was fascinated by the prominent veins in her hands and forearms, and by how she wore her black hair piled up. Her shade of lipstick, her gold-loop earrings, and her double string of pearls made her more *chic* than all the other young women of my acquaintance. She smoked cigarettes, not because she enjoyed tobacco, but only to give the final touch to an image of elegance that was rare in the tropics.

We were married in the cathedral at Puerto Cangrejo. Rosalba encouraged me to read the great European writers, to know classical music, and to insert myself into the life of our city in ways beyond my business affairs. The local hospital was struggling and I was asked to organize a fund-raising event. It wasn't long before I was elected president of its board.

6

Jaime Pineda was Cecil's nephew. Their family—pawns in the violent history of several empires battling over four centuries—had come to the Republic from a British island in the Caribbean, and they were the descendants of African slaves brought over to toil in the plantations.

Fucho Pineda, Jaime's father, was a big, strapping, handsome banana worker with an enormous black moustache. His death by stabbing in the far plantations across the mountains remained an unsolved mystery.

Jaime was José Miguel's age, and when he turned thirteen Cecil asked if I would put his nephew to work in the *Ferreteria*. He could sweep floors; he could carry out garbage.

The boy was intelligent and eager to please, and he grew tall and lithe. Soon I assigned him to the stock room where he learned to keep our inventory in good order. His lips were thick and dark, his skin the color of coffee with a drop of cream. Catlike in his movements, he loved to dance. He was honest and open-faced, and later became a favorite of women who were charmed by his candor.

Jaime did a fine job in the *Ferreteria*, grasping easily all of the many details of ordering, storing, and selling. He hummed to himself, smiling in his work, and he was deferential to me. He tried to be friendly to my son, but José Miguel snubbed him.

Jaime did very well in school, but continued working part of each day for us. He was an excellent truck driver and delivered supplies to builders in the countryside. I trusted him completely with materials and receipts. I would give him money and never had to check his arithmetic.

We didn't talk about his uncle, but I always had the feeling that young Pineda was the only one who really understood Cecil. I could sense a quiet admiration in each for the other—the uncle for the intelligence and energy of the nephew, and an unspoken pride in the nephew for the uncle's manliness.

Eventually Jaime enrolled part-time in the Agricultural College, but even then, when he was becoming more focused on his studies, he was able every week to find hours to help us working at the *Ferreteria*.

Much lip service is given to the concept of democracy in Puerto Cangrejo. The Republic was born out of a fierce nineteenth century struggle against Spanish autocracy, and no one ever dared publically to doubt the essential truth of the high ideals put forth by the American and French revolutions. However, realists don't ignore the obvious differences between people. Some qualities are inherited, and it is best to accept that. Different classes have different roles in a society.

During my student years in the States I saw quickly that, in fact, the ideal of equal treatment didn't exist in daily American life. The U.S. proclaims its benevolence and justice for all, but only a fool fails to notice how some have more, and some have less.

So it is in the Republic—and everywhere in the world. Although it's hard for Americans to understand that class exists even in a place where most of the people are racially mixed, being naïve is no help to anyone. In Puerto Cangrejo, a person judged to be Negro is excluded from the Swim and Tennis Club, even though many of the members themselves have physical features fitting the definition of *Negro*. That's the way things are. I didn't question it. Neither did others in our circle.

The Republic has a small minority of citizens who are purely European by inheritance. Don Marinero had no trouble being accepted into that group, and our family lived accordingly. It wasn't a question of skin color, but rather of intelligence, energy, and education. Thus, Arab families—newcomers like the Nasrifs—fit comfortably into the Republic's highest social class.

I do not apologize for it. I merely state a fact. We worked hard and knew we had a good life, but we were not free from worry. It was impossible not to be aware of subliminal resentments beneath the surface of things in daily life, and we could never be certain that the social lines would last into the future. There were abortive attempts by communists to change things. Protests for land reform, for higher wages, for better care at the government hospital where I tried to improve things. But then it would all cool down, and life went on as before.

7

Like a dull ache that one has almost, but not quite successfully, conjured out of one's mind, the relationship our son had with the daughter of Vargas-Macayo remained for me—especially in the hours of the night—not painful, but menacing.

Rosalba and I resisted bringing it up, but there were times when we couldn't avoid it, and then more or less cut off the subject with shrugs. José Miguel, we told each other, was young. It was in the nature of things that some rebellion was not only to be expected, but probably healthy. There was nothing more to say. His good sense would prevail.

What was truly terrible continued to be the lengthening distance between José Miguel and us. All we encountered was sullen silence.

And then came more news.

"Can it be true?" Rosalba asked.

"No, of course not."

"But . . ."

"You've seen her," I shook my head. "She's a slut, a little tramp. Who knows how many men have had her?"

"But people talk."

"Let them."

"José Miguel looks pale, doesn't he?"

"No."

"I'm worried about him."

"No one will believe her. It's her word against his."

"And her father?"

Rafael Salazar's words came back to me.

Just let Vargas-Macayo know . . . that you respect him as a man . . . give consideration to what he says . . . You needn't agree . . . let him know that you are listening . . .

A fleeting twinge of guilt about ignoring Rafael's advice evolved into a dull sense of unease.

"I don't fear him," I told my wife. "And you shouldn't either."

In fact, I did fear a visit from the girl's father, but if he had a complaint against my son he never sought me out. Somehow with those people illegitimacy seems the rule.

Dean or no Dean, I thought, he can't escape his true background. If the child is José's, good luck for the Vargas-Macayo family. It will improve their genetic stock.

A week later a visitor came to see me. I was about to leave the *Ferreteria* for lunch at home when my old school friend, Umberto Dominguez, arrived. Umberto, the tallest man in Puerto Cangrejo, is the commandant at the airport barracks, and he had to duck his head stepping into my office. I hadn't met up with him for several months and seeing him in his crisp Colonel's uniform brightened my spirits.

"I'm happy to see you, *amigo*," I said. "*Qué pasa?*"

"A bit of information you should have, *Toño*." He smiled faintly. "Our friend Vargas-Macayo will be stepping down from his duties at the college."

"Oh?"

"I don't have details. There's talk of a health problem, but some say he's been thinking about retiring for a while."

"You're a good friend to tell me."

"I know you like to keep up with things."

"Indeed, and I'm grateful for your courtesy."

"*Con mucho gusto.*"

The news traveled quickly and the first small protests were respectful and orderly. Only a few students stood quietly with posters at the entrance to the Agricultural College, and I was upset to see that Jaime Pineda was one of them.

> *Restore Dean Vargas-Macayo.*

> *The Oligarchy has gone too far.*

The crowds grew in size and began repetitive chanting in unison:

> *Vargas-Macayo, sí! Tirania, no!*

> *Oligarquía es despotismo!*

The expressed sentiments were not news to me, but I was frightened by the speed of the response and the numbers, not only of protesting students, but ordinary townspeople. How did it grow so quickly? And how stupid Jaime Pineda was to participate in it.

I was sure that the whole thing had been planned in advance, and even that Vargas-Macayo himself had a big part in organizing it. People seemed to assume immediately that his departure was not a retirement, but a firing, and once again Rafael Salazar's words came back to me.

> . . . *be more open-minded, Antonio . . . he's no fool . . . students worship him . . . a real leader, a man with appeal . . .*

8

Several days later, at one o'clock in the morning, a single rifle shot fired through the open window of his kitchen killed Vargas-Macayo. He had been sitting at a table with a pile of books and an ancient Royal typewriter before him. The bullet struck him in the back and he fell forward, spattering blood on the opposite wall and soaking the paper he was writing, from which it dripped to form a large irregular pool on the floor.

The news spread instantly through Puerto Cangrejo. There were bursts of gunfire and explosions in the night. At three in the morning crowds of people were already on the streets. By sunrise ordinary townspeople carrying placards were everywhere. The police pushed them away from the stores, but students began throwing rocks. Windows were smashed not far from *Ferreteria Nasrif.*

For two days we did not venture outside, but from our windows we could tell what was going on in the streets. It wasn't good.

The usual daily requests for food by people who begged at our door had ceased. After the shooting began it was just as well that they no longer came. Despite some confidence that the rebellion would be put down quickly, I had no patience for beggars then. My father had called them the "meek ones", and now I found myself thinking about him, a man without a trace of self-doubt.

"The first generation makes the fortune and the second makes use of it," Don Marinero told me more than once. "The third pisses it away."

It was during those days that I began to have a recurring dream about an empty house. I would wake from it with a tight residue of loneliness that faded only if I kept busy, but being cooped up indoors made that nearly impossible.

Three evenings after the murder there was a knock at our door. I could see someone standing in the street below.

"Who's there?" I called.

"Jaime Pineda, Don Antonio. May we talk?"

"Not now."

"Then, tomorrow? At what time tomorrow?"

"What do you want?"

"What time tomorrow?"

"Go away, Pineda."

He stepped away from the building and retreated down the street.

In the morning the streets were quiet, and I went to the *Ferreteria*. There was shredded paper and garbage along the sidewalks and broken glass in the street, but nothing had been touched at our place. There were even a few customers inside and Pineda was taking care of them. I went into my office and looked at the pile of accumulated bills and correspondence.

At noon Pineda locked the place and came to stand at my door.

"May we talk now?" he asked.

"What is it, Pineda?"

"I'm sorry all this is happening," he said.

"Permit me to doubt that."

"I know you saw me holding a poster a few days ago."

"Indeed."

"I want you to know that people suspect José Miguel."

"What are you talking about?"

"You know that Estrellita Vargas-Macayo is pregnant?"

"So I've heard."

"People think José Miguel is the father . . ."

"Don't talk nonsense."

"No one knows for sure . . ."

"Please . . . spare me."

"They also say he murdered her father."

"You fool! Get out of my office."

He didn't move. "No," he said. "You will listen." He came forward, pulled a chair from the corner very close to me, and sat down.

"Get out of here! Get out!"

"Don't be foolish, Don Antonio. This is a big problem for you."

I was stunned by his self-possession.

"Do you understand that people are wanting to punish someone?" he searched my face. "There is talk of getting rid of José Miguel. Do you see? They think he is not a good person. He is spoiled, he is rude to people. He is too proud, too unkind."

"I will have you arrested, Pineda."

"No, you won't. You will listen. You and I can have an agreement— something that will be good for both of us. I can help keep José Miguel safe. You can help me."

I stood up suddenly. It was all I could do to keep from striking him.

"Calm yourself, Don Antonio. All I'm asking is that you listen to my offer."

"Your offer? Your offer? Who do you think you are? You're some ignorant trash, and you're offering me something?"

"Look, that's exactly the problem here, isn't it? You consider me trash."

"What are you talking about? I've been good to you, helped you, treated you well . . ."

"That's the only reason I've decided to help you, Don Antonio."

I sat down, infuriated, but wanting to end the discussion as quickly as possible.

"Fine, what's your offer. Be quick about it."

"Very simple," he said. "This is a revolution. Things will not go back to the way they have been."

I attempted a smile. "Don't be so sure," I said.

"No, things have already changed. The people are fed up. They want real progress. They don't believe it will come if an oligarchy of wealthy people, people like your family, continue to exercise power while the rest of us work like dogs."

I shook my head in disbelief, but he continued.

"I can make sure that José Miguel will be safe, and that you and your wife can be taken to a safe place . . ."

"What are you saying?"

"Perhaps Belize," Jaime said. "You will have to leave the Republic."

"You have some nerve!"

"Don Antonio, even if this revolution is put down by the army, things will not go back to the way they have been. You are much better off leaving here. In return for guaranteeing your safe escape from here, I will ask you to sign some papers that give me the ownership of several properties."

"Get out of here! You must think I'm crazy."

"No, I'm sure you're a very sensible man," he went on. "That's why this should be quite easy to understand. We could simply end the discussion right here without an agreement. The result of that would be that a mob will take José Miguel and will kill him for the murder of Vargas-Macayo. He won't be given a trial, but he will be judged guilty because he had a reason for killing that man. I do not know what Vargas-Macayo threatened him with for ruining Estrellita's reputation, but it doesn't really matter to me, and it certainly won't matter to the people who run in the streets and break windows with stones."

"I don't believe this."

"Don Antonio, just sign these papers. Cecil, my uncle, will take you, your wife, and José Miguel by boat to Belize. You won't need the farm. Cecil will run it from now on. I will take care of *Ferreteria Nasrif.* I will even be willing to keep that name. And we have plans for the distillery, and the trucking business, too. Everything has been decided. We can accomplish it without the signing of papers, but it will be neater, much neater, if it's all done cleanly. Don't you agree?"

Here in Miami, to keep my mind from exploding with anger and fear, I write like a crazy man. What will become of us? Will this be the end?

I choke with frustration at my surrender to Jaime Pineda. He was nothing when his uncle asked me to take him on. Nothing—a miserable urchin with a life before him like that of all the others, a future of hunger, work, insecurity, illness, desperation, and alcohol. But he grabbed that chance, and didn't waste it. And so, mingled with my rage and sorrow, there is also bitter admiration. Pineda and José Miguel are the same age.

9

In the first days of the rebellion I was mostly worrying about my wife and son. Terror held the city, and Rosalba's spirit had contracted and withered. She had been a proud woman, but suddenly seemed unable even to utter words, just soft tearful mouthing. It tore at me.

José Miguel was spirited away by Cecil who would only say that my son was in a safe place. "At the right moment I will bring him to my boat. I will come to get you. We will go to Belize. But, remember: right now he is a fugitive. He is wanted for the murder of Vargas-Macayo."

It was almost impossible not to feel hopeless. José Miguel's life depended on Cecil's competence and loyalty, but despite wanting to put it all outside myself in a realm of not knowing, I was tormented by the thought that for too long my son had been beyond my reach.

All of our servants except for Cruz, the mulatto cook, had deserted when the shooting began. We could hear them slipping away in the night, making small hushed sounds like mice scurrying behind walls. Only Cruz stayed, sullen and pregnant. And why? Loyalty? Not likely. She had been brought from the farm as a young girl and had been taught to serve, but one never knew with these people. None of them could be trusted. There had always been a fear that one of them, or more than one, might turn on the family that had given them sustenance for years.

Beggars began coming to the door again. The "meek ones." Duplicitous hangers-on, scavengers, I thought. Let them go to the Devil. Whatever meager concern I felt for the common people of the city clung as an inauthentic fragment of what Don Marinero had attempted to teach me. I had no time for them. We had done our part. It was too late now. Look what had happened. It served them right.

Although Cecil's plan seemed our only chance, there was another possibility. As soon as the Army sent in the necessary troops things could get back to normal. Umberto Dominguez stopped by one morning.

"It is going to be short-lived, Don Antonio. A minor disturbance," he said. "We shall cut them out like a surgeon excising a cancer."

But what was taking so long? All through the days the crack of intermittent rifle fire and cries and smoke had filled the streets of the port and so few people had ventured out that it was as if the city had been abandoned. Looking out through a space between drawn curtains, the scene appeared devoid of life and the unfamiliar wasted neighborhood sickened me. Part of a smashed concrete wall hung by what looked like a few wires from the frame of a building opposite. A carcass torn by wolves, I thought. Alone and helpless, even the sunshine seemed driven away by fear and death.

Fires were set and bombs ripped open a warehouse where some of our trucks were garaged. The leftists took the power station at Refugio and immobilized operations at the fruit company by cutting off the electricity. From our second floor window I could see the deserted long wharf where bananas lay rotting in the heat. No ship had put in for a week.

At nightfall the people remained behind bolted doors and shuttered windows. The only lights were tentative flickers of candles in the gloom, while far away one could make out the orange glow of fires on the hillside where the Army had a small encampment.

I heard the murmur of Rosalba's praying. She had been there in the back bedroom for two days, mumbling for the safety of our son. How many times had we argued about the proper way to raise this difficult child? For Rosalba the approach had always been more love, while to me that seemed beside the point. Of course I loved my son, but there was responsibility, too. And while harsh discipline had never been my way, I had followed each phase in José Miguel's life with quiet, suppressed dismay. When I thought about it now it hurt me to realize that I had no common interest with my son and only heir. For José Miguel, life was cockfights and whores. Now he was a priority target of the leftists. A fugitive. A suspected murderer.

With Friday's dawn an ominous quiet came over Puerto Cangrejo. Gunfire ceased, and in the brief tepid hour before the sun began to bear down with its full metallic glare, a few of the meek ones made their way cautiously from one doorway to the next until they came to the iron gate that guarded the entrance to our house. Always hungry and never having more food than they could eat at once, they came to their patron. They trusted that I would sustain them, even now with my many troubles. Maybe a bag of melons, or perhaps a covered dish of warmed beans. The custom of giving food had begun with my father who had been poor himself. The faces of the meek ones changed from time to time, but there were always poor people to feed, people who had done small jobs and favors for the family.

"They come, Don Antonio. They are here for the food." Cruz stood at the window holding her hands over her swollen belly, a dark blot of perspiration on the upper part of her pale blue dress. She looked questioningly at me.

"Give them something," I said. "But don't let them come up; make them wait in the hallway." Cruz gripped the banister and eased down the long flight of stairs.

I paced nervously, glancing toward the open door of my son's room. I could see the cabinet with the treasured seashells and the old toys that hadn't been played with for years. I lit a cigarette and blew the smoke out quickly with fury and exasperation. I could hear the murmurs of the people as they waited for Cruz to bring food. So quiet, I thought, after the terror of yesterday.

And where is the "surgeon" Umberto Dominguez promised? What is the Army doing? Why are they not patrolling the streets? Things were utterly confused and out of control.

I sat down, and immediately thoughts came to me of my haunting nightmare—an empty house.

Then I heard the sound of bare feet padding up the stairs.

"Cecil!" I cried.

The tall, gray haired Negro wearing dirty shorts and a straw hat appeared. The whites of his eyes shone luminously in the dim room. His head nearly touched the ceiling.

"What the hell, Cecil—what are you doing here?"

"It's time," he said, stooping toward me. He spoke gravely and without servility. The boat was hidden in the estuary and no one had seen them. José Miguel was on board. "We should leave tonight, but the carburetor's broken down."

"My son . . ?"

"José Miguel broke his arm. He fell while he was running."

"Oh, God!"

"Yes, he was running away, but I've strapped it up in a sling."

"Oh, Jesus." I hit my fists together. The black man watched me for a long moment.

"This kind of fight's not for him," said Cecil. "I mean . . . it ain't no cockfight."

"You shut up, Cecil." I glared at him. "You fix that engine. What do you need?"

"I'm just saying this is a war."

"So what."

I pulled out a large wad of folded currency from my pocket. "What side are you on, Cecil?"

"Maybe the Army won't come, Don Antonio."

"Never mind. Fix the carburetor. How long will it take?" I handed him a few bank notes. He held it in his hand and looked around the room.

"I don't know, maybe a few hours. The lines may be plugged. If they are I'll have to rig a sail."

"Do it," I snapped. "Send word back by one of your boys. I want to know exactly when you're ready to leave."

The ceiling fan hung motionless. I mopped my brow and cursed Cecil's broken-down boat. The surly black bastard, I thought.

Now, somewhere toward the south, I thought I could hear bursts of rifle fire. I moved to the window and held away the curtain to see the sky darkening and a few early drops of rain falling into the dust. At the corner a trio of soldiers guarded the gas station, but their posture was slack and I knew they were drunk and useless as protection. It was the seventh day of the rebellion. The yellow posters were still glued to the street lamps where the students had pasted them. The headline in black ink burned in my mind.

THE OLIGARCHY IS FINISHED.

I knew the words by heart. *"A wealthy few . . . mostly foreigners . . . not content with our hospitality . . . enemies of the people . . . the poor, the sick, the uneducated . . . conniving evil-doers allied with the repressive inhuman capitalists of the American fruit company . . ."*

Suddenly the rain began in earnest. First, a breeze coming up, cooling my skin; then the palms below slapping and creaking; and finally the drumming of rain on the tin roof, needles of water hitting it hard like buck-shot.

"Antonio," Rosalba called to me from the bedroom. I stood in the doorway, sensible of her thin body on the bed, exhausted by days of weeping.

"The noise . . ."

"It's only the rain, my dear."

"Are there guns, too?"

"A while ago, but they've stopped." I got down beside her and we lay together for several minutes without speaking. I took her hand and kissed it. The rain battered from above and the air was close and warm. She murmured something quietly.

"What did you say?"

"Miami," she said. "We will have to go there. We can't stay here."

"I thought the Army would come, Rosalba, but Cecil was here. He thinks we should leave tonight."

I heard the doubt in my own voice.

"It's like a punishment," she said wearily.

In the dim room my dream came back—the large, empty house beckoning me. On the outside it looked inviting, and I was walking toward it. I felt anticipation going into the comfort and security of the rooms, but as I passed through the front door the interior of the house dissolved, and I stood bereft in an empty shell of four walls.

"Punishment," Rosalba repeated. She held my hand lightly, weakly.

I sat up and reached into my pocket for the cigarettes, but I'd left them in the parlor.

"No, don't go."

"I'm not going to listen to your blame," I said softly, pulling away. "We have helped these people. My father helped them and I have helped them. We have done nothing wrong."

"But, José Miguel . . ."

"José Miguel got that girl pregnant, but he didn't murder her father. Vargas-Macayo was a troublemaker and a fool. The Army killed him."

I stood up and left the room. At the window I looked down at the drenched town. The rain had already stopped, but the sky was still gray and the downpour had turned the street into a canal. I saw a rat swimming along in the slow current, its small head pointing the way. The guns were beginning again, closer it seemed, and on the horizon there were flashes of lightning. I lit another cigarette and went back into the bedroom. Rosalba reached out to me and I lay down next to her again.

"I'm sorry," she said.

"No, you're right," I sighed.

Fifty thousand dollars in a Miami bank account, I thought. That is all we shall have. I knew Miami with its glitter and crowds. Fifty thousand wouldn't go far. I thought about the distillery with its great vats of fermenting juice. I thought about the farm and all it had meant to me.

The shouting in the street woke me. I sprang to the window and saw Cecil, his back to the gate, arguing with six students. The Negro towered over them.

"Go home," he said quietly. "You'll do no good here."

They stood their ground, taunting and joking.

"Why are you protecting him?" asked one who was juggling a stone.

"Get lost," said Cecil, smiling and turning from them with a wave of his hand. He knocked at the gate. I heard Cruz open it and saw the students move away. The sky was darker and a small gust of wind stirred the palms. Rosalba came into the parlor as Cecil reached the top of the stairs, and I cast a brief glance at her to judge her mood.

"Is the boat fixed?" I asked. I knew Rosalba would be annoyed at how Cecil leaned against the wall, wiping his forehead with a dirty handkerchief. The Negro regarded both of us and nodded.

Rosalba took my hand. "Tell him, Antonio," she said. "Tell him we're leaving."

I could see Cruz standing in the kitchen doorway, a dishtowel in her hand. Outside the rolling sound of thunder boomed far up the coast.

"Cecil," I began. "When can we leave?"

The black man smiled. "You need old Cecil now, don't you?"

My eyes widened. "My family has done you many favors, Cecil."

"Yes, I know. Your father did, but you were never the man he was," Cecil went on, spitting out the words. "And your son with his cockfights and women. He lost his nerve. You're finished. I think I hate you the most. I hate your guts, but I'll get you out."

And then we were all on the boat. Only Cruz had remained in the house. "Don't worry," she'd said, a tired note in her voice. "I'll take care of everything." Rosalba had kissed her and I saw tears in Cruz's eyes.

False tears, I thought. That she would possess my home enraged me. Sickened me. Three generations of our family had lived here. I had been born in this house. Don Marinero had died in this very room.

Forget it, I told myself, squeezing my eyes tightly.

Forget it.

My breath came with difficulty as we followed Cecil running through the streets to the creek and then along the path that wound into the estuary. White birds roosted up in the trees, motionless, their still forms ghostlike in the night. We found José Miguel weak and frightened, but in no real danger. Soon we would be in Belize. Then we would fly to Miami where there would be a doctor for his arm.

The boat moved through the black water, its hull brushing against reeds and the put-put sound of its slowly turning engine coughing into the warm air. When we reached the sea a breeze came up, and the little boat rocked into the waves. We stood silently, gripping the rail. Puerto Cangrejo lay dimly behind, its outlines showing as vague gray shapes against the darker night.

Cecil's invective rankled. There he stood, black and hulking above us at the wheel. Damn him, I thought.

We *were* finished . . . by a mob of ignorant, lazy, ungrateful riffraff.

My father's idea about the generations was facile and simplistic. Or was he right? I had certainly built things up and had tried to do my best. Or was everything inevitable? And did I have an equal share with my son in ruining things?

José Miguel sat leaning against the side of the little wheelhouse, eyes closed and his free hand steadying the broken forearm in the sling Cecil had made. Even after all the disagreements with my son, and despite my deep disappointment in how he had turned out, the sight of his suffering affected me.

I couldn't control myself and began to sob.

Far off down the coast a few lights shone and my wet eyes changed them into magnified sparkling stars.

Rosalba clutched at my arm. "Don't," she said to me. "Don't."

All was lost.

I only wanted to cry out.

Up on the Hill

A PICK-UP TRUCK CAME ALONG the lake road and turned into the gravel driveway that led to the big colonial house. At the top of the hill the driver jumped out and went up on the columned porch to ring the bell.

He was a neat little man in faded jeans and an Eisenhower army jacket, and as he stood listening and waiting for someone to come he turned from side to side and surveyed the gray clapboard siding and the white shutters that gleamed in the afternoon's autumn sun.

Something about him spoke of anxiety or apprehension. His eyes darted here and there, moving ceaselessly and giving him the look of one who doubts that there is any inherent stability in things. When a shadow moved behind the curtained window he stepped closer to the threshold, his nose just inches from the brass knocker, but his head pulled back as the door was opened by a tall pale man wearing an ascot and tweed jacket.

"Hello, Doc," said the visitor.

"Oh, Al," said Doc, retreating a step. "Was it today?"

"I think it was today, Doc, but I can wait. Do you have something going on?"

Doc turned to look behind him.

"No, no," he said. "I was just sitting here. Come in. You had some difficulty you wanted to discuss?"

"No real difficulty, Doc. I don't want to barge in. If you and Gloria . . ."

"She's lying down just now," said Doc. He led the way through the hall into the living room.

"It's been a long time since we seen each other," Al said.

"I know. Things are a little different now."

The living room extended the full length of the house. At the far end was a large picture window overlooking the lake.

"Sit there on the couch," said Doc. "You can see the water." He pulled up a rocking chair and faced Al.

"What's up?"

"I just thought I would ask your advice, Doc. It's about my kid. I've been kind of worried about him."

"What's wrong?'

Al leaned forward, but the light was coming in from the lake and he could only see the outline of Doc's head. The face was in shadow.

"Ruth's got him," Al struggled with the words. "And that's bad enough . . . but I think that creep, Wayne, is back, and the kid has been running away. The police have called me a couple of times."

Doc's rocker creaked on the oak floor.

"What else?"

"I'm afraid I'm going to do something crazy, Doc. I don't want to. I really don't. But I've been thinking about shooting that fucking bastard."

Doc stood up, turning, and looked out at the lake. He folded his arms over his chest.

"I know Ruth's a rotten mother, Doc, but Tom's never run away before. I think that lousy Wayne has been roughing him up."

"Have you talked to the lawyer?"

"That jerk? I'm sorry, Doc. I know he's your pal, but I'll never trust that guy again."

Doc turned to face Al again. He smiled briefly.

"Would you like some beer?"

"Sure."

Doc went into the kitchen and Al wandered around looking at things. Shelves filled with books; the small piano; lamps; paintings on the walls.

"What does Ruth say?" Doc called from the kitchen.

"She's never there, Doc. Same old story. Once a whore, always a whore."

Al ran his hand over the polished surface of an end table. "How's everything working out with you and Gloria?" he called out.

"Fine. You know women, Al. Sometimes you have to let them know where you stand."

Al smiled as he heard the refrigerator door slam. There was a sharp click of metal as the beer was being opened. Doc came back into the living room with two cans and handed one to Al.

"Cheers."

Al gave Doc a cautious look and grinned. "Cheers, Doc."

"What do you want me to do, Al?"

"Maybe talk to Tommy . . . about school and all. You know he would respect you. The kid is smarter than me or Ruth. He has no one to guide him, inspire him. Maybe you could talk some sense into him."

Doc sipped his beer.

"Doc, you know my temper. Sometimes I can't talk to the kid. And I feel like bustin' Ruth for everything she's done. I'm not going to, Doc, but sometimes I really want to hurt her."

Doc stood up again and paced the room. "What else have you been up to, Al?"

"Oh, a little carpentry in town," said Al, leaning forward, elbows on knees. "Some cabinets this week. Got a paint job out in Thomaston starting tomorrow."

"You'd better watch it, Al. You'll get rich working so hard and you won't like it."

"Fat chance," said Al. "How about you, Doc? Since Gloria moved in I hardly see you."

"I know . . . it's not like before."

"I miss our talks. We had some real good talks."

"We did." Doc pulled out a clean white handkerchief, sat down, and blew his nose. He raised his eyebrows and looked over at Al.

"And we had some good times, Doc."

"I remember, Al."

"What about fishing? Do any fishing lately, Doc?"

"No."

"Just working, huh?"

"Yes."

"I see your car in front of the office all the time, so I know you're there seeing your patients, but I never see you."

"I'm usually around here."

"How's it going with you and Gloria?"

Doc was tilting back in his chair, passing his hand over his eyes. He leaned forward and looked down as if he saw something in the corner of the room.

"I always like coming here," Al went on, ignoring Doc's silence and looking over at the bookshelves. "I remember that first time, right after you moved up here from the City and you asked me to look the place over to see about painting it."

"You did a good job, Al."

"I remember what you said. *You're a great find, Al. Old school. Screw the unions.*"

"I was just being a wise guy." Doc drained his can of beer and stood up. "I'll get some more," he said. He was unsteady and slipped a little, but regained his balance.

Al went out on the deck overlooking the lawn that sloped down to the lake. Clouds moved across the sun and a chill came over him. A little raft floated about twenty yards off shore. Doc came back with the beer and they leaned against the railing.

"What a beautiful place, Doc. I always loved it, even when I was a kid. There was no house here then—just the hill and the trees and the water."

"Well," said Doc. "Things change, don't they? Anything wrong with that?"

"No, Doc. No. Remember that time we were down on the raft and what you said?" asked Al.

"What I said? About what?"

"About how sometimes you would catch yourself thinking about how you actually owned this place now and that you had a picture of it in your mind. You said it was an image of lying on the raft with a beautiful chick and a tray of gin and tonics. And how it would look through a camera, shooting up toward the house. A guy like you, and the girl, and the drinks . . . and the lake and the lawn and the big house on the hill. How it would make a great ad for a company that makes gin."

Al laughed and looked over at Doc, but Doc wasn't listening. He was just sitting on the bench staring out at the lake with a doleful look on his face.

"Hey, Doc. Anything I can do for you?" Al sat down next to Doc and put his hand on his arm.

"Do?"

"You know, as a friend. We had a lot in common before. Both of us being divorced and all."

Doc stared down at the deck.

"I learned a lot from you, Doc."

"Really? What?"

"About what books to read. And about France."

"Yes. Oh, well."

"Something wrong?"

"No."

"How's the Packard? I thought I'd see it in the driveway when I came up."

"It's in the garage."

"Yeah . . . nineteen forty, right? I remember you liked having it there in the driveway, all polished and sharp." Al shook Doc's arm gently. "Remember?"

"Yes. I did."

Al put his beer down and got up to go to the toilet.

"Nature calls," he said.

He went into the house and walked down the hall. The bedroom door was closed, but he heard a sound.

He stopped.

A moan . . . the sound of someone moaning.

The porch door slammed again and Al turned. Doc came into the hall.

"I thought I heard someone in there," said Al.

Doc said nothing, his pale face in shadow.

Al froze.

There were footsteps in the room, and suddenly someone fell against the door from the inside.

It burst open, and a woman lurched into the hall. Her face was smeared with clotted blood, and she stood hanging on to the doorknob. Her eyes wavered, squinting in the dim light, then focused on Al's face.

"Jesus, Gloria," Al whispered.

"He knocked me out," said Gloria.

Al turned to face Doc, whose figure, shoulders slumped, filled the space at the end of the hall.

"Jesus," Al whispered.

The woman's face came very close to his. Like a clown's, the skin showed white next to the smudges of blood.

"He knocked me out."

"Holy Christ."

Doc's tall figure turned away, but he fell back against the wall and slowly slid lower until he was sitting on the floor. He looked like a little boy.

"Hey, Doc!"

Doc was looking down at the carpet. His face was hidden, but he was moving his head from side to side.

"Hey, Doc . . . you okay?"

Al wanted to understand. What would he see in Doc's face? Disapproval? Disavowal? Incomprehension?

Then Doc looked up, and Al saw the tears streaming down his cheeks.

NEXT TIME

WHEN JOEL SAW HER it was just as a thin splash of red against a dark background. He was sitting in the top row of the grandstand looking out over all the people and he strained forward to be sure. Could it be?

He watched as she moved up in the queue. From her rounded shoulders he caught a hint of the sensual languor that he remembered. In a few minutes he was able see her face and it was unchanged. She still wore glasses with that style of clear plastic frames that everyone wore in those days. Her clear, olive-toned skin was unchanged. Her hair, black and short with a small curl at the end, even had the sheen that he knew. The dark red jersey dress clung softly although he couldn't tell about her figure—just that she was rather tall.

Marcia . . .

She had loved him once.

Somewhere down in the milling crowd were his wife, his children, and his parents. The day was bright and sunny, and a happy confusion of muted voices and laughter drifted up to him, but there was hardly any air movement and even with all the people it was strangely still. Everything seemed embedded in cotton.

The police had fenced off Central Park West with long portable wood barriers—white boards with black stripes that looked like stick drawings of zebras. The queue was long. He couldn't see its end, and it moved slowly forward as the people waited their turn to get a seat.

Every few moments he thought he saw one of his kids darting somewhere in the crowd.

The trees looked lovely—sycamores they were—with shaggy bark, light green leaves and little spiky seed balls.

She was closer now. For a moment he looked away, and then quickly back again to test his small doubt. Thinking of her was always tinged with guilt. A long time ago, in youth, friends had told him she was his if he only wanted her, but that was at a time when he loved Zoe.

No, it wasn't to be.

Zoe, of course, was unattainable and loved by four or five young men. She would flirt with Joel for a few weeks, then with Paul, then Glenn, then back to Joel. Most people thought she really loved Paul. Misery had been the theme of that year and Joel remembered vividly Zoe's hot cheek when they danced in someone's darkened basement to *Little White Lies*. There was a joke about little white lice, and they would break apart ever so slightly to smile, even laugh, each time the phrase came in the song.

And then a few weeks later at another party he would see Zoe dancing with Paul, her face flushed, and clinging, and he would feel a stab of pain. When she danced with Glenn she crossed her fingers, a signal that she wanted someone to cut in. She was losing interest in Glenn. Joel wondered if she ever used this treachery behind his back, too.

He had planned to invite Zoe to the Senior Prom, but he was too late. She was going to the prom with Calvin, a boy who lived in Port Washington and went to Choate.

So, Joel had asked Marcia. He knew she was waiting for him, and she gladly accepted. It was a sultry night in June. They danced in the gym, and the doors were thrown wide open to let in a little breeze. The boys suffered in tuxedos and shoes that didn't fit. The girls were lovely in their gowns of taffeta and tulle. Marcia had a dreamy look all evening and Joel even thought she was beautiful the way she looked at him as they stood waiting for the next number to begin. She had very smooth arms and her skin felt cool. A blue light swept around the darkened gym and colored sparkles flashed from bracelets and necklaces. The band thudded and blared and couples swept slowly by.

Somewhere at home—on the top shelf of the linen closet in the hall, or perhaps in a dusty box in the garage—he had a photograph of four of them at the Casa Granada, the roadhouse where they went after the prom. The picture showed them sitting around a table, all looking straight at the camera. Marcia was sitting very close to him, half-resting her head on his shoulder, and he appeared rather smug.

He had the family car that night, and as they drove home in the early morning hours the other couple cuddled in the back seat.

When he took Marcia to her door she kissed him passionately, held him for a long moment, then broke away, and turned just before stepping into the house.

"Next time let someone else drive," she said.

Down in the crowd some people were beginning to drift away. Joel could see her very close to the part of the grandstand where she would begin to disappear from his view. People alongside him were leaving and he stood up. Stepping over a few empty rows, he made his way down through the mob to the pavement and walked quickly toward the line of people. She saw him and he was alongside her in seconds. Gently, he took her by the wrist just as she was going under the stand. She looked up at him without a word and came along easily with him as they left the crowd and finally reached the sidewalk. She was expressionless, but he wanted to kiss her.

"What happened?" he asked her.

She was silent. There was sadness in her bearing, a limp and subdued quality that made his heart break. A thousand questions flooded his mind, but if he voiced them they would be muffled by the stillness and the peculiar heaviness in the air.

She mystified him, and he thought about how she had once loved him. Now she was sophisticated—probably a career woman. What did she do? He had to find out what she had done, who she was.

"I don't even know what you do," he said, afraid that she would move away. He imagined that she was famous. "You might be a neurosurgeon for all I know. Or managing editor of *The New Yorker*. I want to find out what you've been doing. It's been such a long time."

He still held her by the arm. Her dress seemed darker, almost black.

"I could see you tonight," she said.

He remembered his wife. Somewhere out in the crowd she would be looking for him. And the children. And his parents. And the Avis rental car. He was from San Diego. This was New York.

"No. I can't tonight. Tell me now. We can talk now. Tell me. What do you do? What are you like?"

He thought of the rental car. Where had he parked it? And the children—they must be around here someplace. Cars were beginning to move along the avenue. They were taking away the striped zebra things. Sunlight shone on a black fender, a brilliant sparkling reflection with long golden rays.

She had stopped talking. She was going away. He held her by the hands.

I'm sorry, he thought.

But he didn't say it.

BOOK OF LIFE

LUKE SPERRY'S FATHER WAS doing two things at once, neither of them very well. He was trying to cut another slice of meat from the roast, but the knife was dull and he was getting red in the face. At the same time, he was talking about free will and how it sets man apart from the beasts.

Luke had heard this before.

This is the way he talks on Meeting nights. All of a sudden he shifts gears to that higher plane.

As he watched his father he saw the lines in the handsome face and the slight hunch of the shoulders, and Luke felt a dark wave of loneliness come over him.

He and his parents had been silent as they finished a light Sunday supper and from the dining room they could see the corner. There was sporadic evening traffic running down the boulevard into Baltimore and cars waited to cross at the light on Aston road. Luke looked away from his father and wondered if he could get out of the house without an argument. It was another Community of Man night. He pushed his salad plate aside and picked up a dessertspoon, running the ball of his thumb along the deep smooth curve.

His mother sat opposite, chewing carefully, with her tired face inclined toward the plate in front of her. She seemed drawn into the act of eating, held there with a tension that annoyed Luke. He looked around the room, at the walls with their floral pattern on yellow and brown paper, at the brass chandelier hanging over the table, and at the maple sideboard standing along the wall. Above it hung a large decorative sunburst made of gold colored metal. It was the symbol of the Community of Man and it made him think of Buddy.

Luke hadn't seen his older brother for two years, and the mystery for him was what living in a commune in New Mexico must be like. Now and then a letter from Buddy would come.

We're brothers and sisters here. We share everything, and everyone is very caring.

So, were they all hippies? What was their dining room like? Maybe it was more like a farmhouse with a big noisy table and girls in Granny dresses. How did they treat someone with a handicap like Buddy's?

Lots of days would go by when he wouldn't think about Buddy, but every so often his brother would appear in a dream. Buddy would be limping along and all of a sudden Luke would wake up in a cold sweat. He had cried the day Buddy left.

"Living on a corner is symbolic," said Luke's father. He pointed to the window. "It constantly reminds me of the moral choices all of us must make."

Luke's mother's face took on a beatific expression. "I've never thought of that before," she said. "What a good connection, Henry! We should mention it to the group."

"I believe I shall," said Luke's father. "By the way, Luke, you'll be here for The Meeting?"

The spoon slipped from Luke's hand and bounced loudly on the floor. "I'm going out," he mumbled, leaning down to retrieve the spoon.

"What did you say? I didn't hear you."

"I said I'm going out."

His father picked up a paper napkin and wiped some brown gravy from his lips. "Where are you going?"

"Over to Margie's."

For a long moment his father and mother looked determinedly at each other.

"Don't her parents get tired of you?" his father asked.

"She's my friend, Dad. They don't care."

How could he explain to them that he wasn't sleeping with Margie; had never so much as kissed her; that she was like a sister? There was no way of approaching that subject with them. No way, even, of beginning, because it touched a thing that was never mentioned in this house, even in a negative way. It was non-existent.

"Luke, you have your own choice to make, too," said his father. "Don't you? About signing?"

Luke stood up. "Can I be excused now?" he asked, looking down at his parents.

"Fine, Luke. It's up to you," said his father, pushing back his chair. "I think you'd enjoy London. But, as I've said before, it's your life."

Luke went into the hall, grabbed his windbreaker, and went out. It was dark now and the chill fall air still smelled of the smoke from the afternoon's leaf fires. There was his Ford parked in the driveway, but he crossed the lawn and began walking down the boulevard in the direction of the school. Better to save the gas. The Ford was turning out to be more expensive to run than he had thought, especially with the goddamn insurance. But, his father had agreed to pay half the premium if he would sign the Book of Life. Talk about choices. Jesus! Sure, he had a choice—turn down the trip to Europe and their gift of half the premium, or sign the damn book and promise them that he would lay off weed and booze and never touch them again. Not that he smoked that much weed—a few joints on weekends. And what harm was there in getting high? It made him more tolerant of people. Brotherhood. He liked getting high and he didn't plan to stop. Sign the Book? He might as well promise to be like them forever.

On the other hand, if he didn't sign the book, it wasn't so much missing the trip or having to pay the whole premium himself. It was much more the disappointment they would feel. They lived for The Community. It was their whole life now, especially after the thing with Buddy. Of course, he knew that had been their own fault, especially the old man's.

Still, Luke thought, can't I, for once in my life, act unselfishly and do something that would please them?

Ahead, dark and dismal on a Sunday night, he saw the school. Across the street was a row of stores and the bowling alley where cars would line up during the week and students would stand around rapping. It was like a tomb now. Some kids whom he knew were leaning against a blue Pontiac, smoking quietly. They saw him and he started to wave, but they turned the other way. Odd, he thought. One of them, Rice, was the son of friends of his parents. They were also members of The Community. In fact, they were probably on their way to The Meeting at his own house right now. Lately, he hadn't had much to do with Rice, but they had been friends in Junior High. Once, at the end of eighth grade, a science teacher had given two white rats to Rice for caretaking during the summer, but the request wasn't appreciated. Rice wanted nothing to do with the rats.

But he was interested in electricity. Luke had a transformer as part of his set of electric trains and Rice asked him to bring it over to his house one day.

"Ever see an electrocution?" Rice had asked.

"What are you going to do?"

Rice connected the wires to the rats' cage. Luke squatted alongside, fascinated. When everything was all set Rice turned the switch—but nothing happened. They fooled around for a while and then Rice had the idea of drowning the rats. Luke winced now as he remembered how they pushed the squirming animals down in a bucket of water until they were still and something white and spongy came floating up.

After that he and Rice didn't see much of each other. It seemed to Luke that Rice had lingered too long in childhood. The cruel streak remained and he became sullen and unfriendly.

Luke walked along the fence by the football field letting the chain links bounce his fingers up and down. The grandstand loomed huge and empty. He had had some great moments on that football field. Isolated, powerful moments when nothing mattered but his speed and his will.

He had talked to Margie about the Book of Life, but she didn't understand. She was too sane—too happy, and too optimistic for a thing like that. Anyway, Jews were different—no matter what anyone said.

He spied a long branch in the gutter and picked it up. It had a certain feel and made a good walking stick. As he poled along he thought back to a year ago when his mother had invited Margie's parents to the Sunday evening meetings. The Bernsteins had come to three or four of them and they had listened politely to the members and to new people like themselves discussing the empty spiritual life of modern man. Luke would sit in the kitchen doing his homework, but he could hear the voices in the living room and could sense the development and resolution of tense moments.

That first time the Bernsteins came his father made a little welcoming speech and suggested going around the room to give each person a chance to say something that had a deeply felt personal meaning. One woman admitted tearfully that she felt upset about her jealousy over her husband's business trips. She had come to the Meeting because she knew she and her husband had to start talking to each other or their marriage would be over. The husband chuckled nervously and said he wished they could both loosen up and enjoy life a little more. A few more people spoke and then it was Luke's father's turn. He cleared his throat and said the most unbelievable thing. He said that he had always known himself to be quite good-looking, that others had told him this, and that, although he knew it was vanity, he had come to accept it as a part of himself. Luke had thought: what a dumb thing to admit! He wondered why the old man didn't talk about Buddy. What could be more personal than your own son whose life you had wrecked? But, then, the old man didn't see it that way and maybe he was right. Maybe Buddy wrecked his own life. Luke couldn't figure his father when he got all hot about religion. He became a different person.

When the Bernsteins had their turn to speak they declined to give out any such personal feelings. They asked if The Community was really non-sectarian. They said they weren't very religious at all, but they didn't hide the fact of being Jewish. That was all they said. There were other newcomers who didn't want to say anything and Luke's mother assured all of them that there was nothing wrong with that; that the purpose of the evening was to give a glimpse into how The Community operated.

It had been founded a decade before by a dentist named Utterbach. At first it was called New World, but the name kept changing. Utterbach had personally taken on the task of forming a grassroots people-to-people movement devoted to a reawakening of man's spirit. By and by, others joined and now several hundred people were members. They even had bumper stickers that said *Man is Holy*. It was supposed to be a non-sectarian movement and Luke had often heard his mother say how important it was that they get some "people of the Jewish faith" to join. He didn't understand why they needed Jews any more than other groups, but that's what his mother said and the old man agreed.

Funny. Luke had first heard the word "kike" from the old man—when he was a little kid.

"What's a kike, Dad?"

"Never mind. Nothing. Forget I said it."

The last Meeting night attended by the Bernsteins was the night the Symbol was explained to the new people. The Symbol was the large gold emblem that appeared to be a sunburst with rays emanating from a central point like a glittering star. All of the rays were fine and narrow except for the vertical and horizontal which were broad and formed a cross.

"This Symbol is universal," said Mr. Sperry to the group. "It incorporates the star, as in Judaism, and the Cross of Jesus, Our Lord. In it are found the unity and diversity of mankind. It's the philosophical basis of true brotherhood. We are many; we are one."

At this Meeting, the final introductory Meeting, new members were asked to accept the Symbol, and to sign the Book of Life. The Bernsteins had said they didn't really want to tie themselves down and that although they agreed with the principles of brotherhood, they didn't feel they should join as they had other commitments.

It was a spooky group all right, Luke thought, as he stood on the bridge over the railroad yard looking down at the tracks. All those freaky types sitting around telling each other about how man needed to be at the center—whatever the hell that meant.

The Sperrys had always belonged to the Episcopal Church and Luke had even had his First Communion when he was in sixth grade. For years they had gone to church every Sunday, but that had come to an end when the troubles with Buddy had started. All those nights with the sounds of his mother screaming and the fights between his father and Buddy. That was back in the days of Vietnam and the hippies. Buddy, who was eight years older than Luke, started to grow his hair long. Luke remembered that Buddy started to smell kind of odd and his eyes were red all the time, but he thought maybe it was because he cried a lot. Buddy would stay in his room with the door locked and the radio blaring The Dead and The Airplane. He was pretty mean and nasty to Luke, too. Little things—like not sharing candy and making Luke get up out of the good chair in the TV room. Then there were the nightly arguments between his mother and father about how to handle Buddy.

Finally the business over the hair came up and that's when all the really bad trouble began. The old man told Buddy to get a haircut and Buddy said he wouldn't. The old man went after him with a scissors and Buddy screamed that he would kill himself if the old man cut his hair off. And that's just about what happened. Buddy was small and wiry, but the old man held him easily and hacked off all that hair. Buddy ran into his room crying and when they broke the door down later that afternoon there were pills lying around and Buddy was barely breathing. Then came the days in the hospital—weeks really. A lot of crying at home and praying of a new kind. Not like in Church. Real, honest praying. Finally Buddy woke up out of his coma and he was alive, but pretty different. He seemed placid and friendly, but his body was twisted so that when he walked he had to pull up his hip and his leg kind of splayed out as he limped along.

Someone inside yelled "Come in!" and Luke opened the door. The aroma of cigar smoke hung in the air of the house. The Bernsteins were sitting around the dining room table with a man and woman Luke didn't know and he very clearly heard his own name spoken in a fragment of the conversation and then the word "community." Three small kids chased one another through the living room, brushed past him, and disappeared into the kitchen. Humboldt was barking and poking his big German shepherd nose into Luke's groin. Margie came out of the dining room.

"They're all in there talking," she said. "Interesting stuff. And there's a great dessert." Her hair was in braids and she wore a sweatshirt, jeans and flip-flops.

"Have you signed it yet!" she whispered.

"Not yet."

"How can you? I mean, they're treating you like a little kid. Worse—they're bribing you."

"Yeah," he said, looking down at his shoes. She put her hand on his arm. "I don't want to hurt them," he went on. "They've never gotten over Buddy. They're convinced drugs caused it all. They don't see. They're old. Frail. You know what I mean?"

"I can't get over how they don't trust you," she said.

"They trust me," he said. "It's a religious thing."

Margie pulled him by the arm into the dining room and her parents introduced him to the other people, Harry and Ann, as

"Margie's friend from school." There was light banter. Mr. Bernstein said his usual thing about how tall Luke was and the other people smiled a lot.

"How are your folks, Luke?" Mrs. Bernstein asked. She observed him with an experimental look as if she were considering going on.

"Oh, fine."

"Tonight is Sunday, isn't it?" she continued. "They must be having one of their Meetings."

"Yeah, they are," he said.

Margie pointed to the cake. "Have some dessert," she said.

They cut him a slice and when he started to eat they went back to their talk and brandy. Mr. Bernstein was enjoying a long, dark-brown cigar. It had an inch and a half of perfect gray ash at the tip.

"So, anyway, Harry, that's how I feel about social life," he said, taking up the thread of the conversation. "And Ann, the trouble with dinner parties is that there are too many people. Once you have more than four or five people . . ."

"You have to be willing to draw people out, Jack," she replied. "You've got to be interested in people."

"Listen, most dinner parties, here's how it goes: what trip did you take? Was the food good? How're your kids doing? My dog has fleas."

Harry was laughing. "I agree with Jack," he said.

Luke ate his cake and Mrs. Bernstein put another piece on his plate. Margie sat alongside him, tilting back her chair. They were asking her about the school and about kids they knew.

"Don't sit like that, Margie," said Mrs. Bernstein.

"How much freedom do you think kids should have, Margie?" asked Ann.

"Complete," said Margie.

"She has it," said Mr. Bernstein.

Margie made a face at her father.

"I'm not kidding," he said. "What can't you do? We don't bother you; you have plenty of freedom."

"Listen," said Harry. "When a girl is seventeen, she's an adult. If she doesn't have an idea of right and wrong by then, she never will. Right, Margie?"

"I guess." Margie looked sideways at Luke and grimaced.

"Look, you have to have trust in them . . . that's all," said Mr. Bernstein, reaching over and grabbing Margie's braids. "We trust you, kid."

Luke chewed and swallowed, and listened. He felt he might be able to stay there forever, bathed in the warmth, letting it wash over him like the benign aroma of the cigar smoke. He sipped the coffee and watched them. There was no secret shame here, no taint.

But a chill sought him out. He could stay here only long enough to take up a little of the warmth. Then came a whiff, a breath of guilt, and the sense that he was betraying his own family. He felt unbalanced as he stood up.

"I have to go," he said.

They all pushed back their chairs and smiled at him. He and Margie went into the living room and stood at the front door.

"I can see you're worried about it," she said.

"Yeah." He put his hand on the doorknob.

"Do you really care about the trip to London?" she asked.

"I don't know."

"Or the money? You could earn that."

"I don't think you see where they're at. You don't know how strongly they feel, how it would hurt them."

"I still say they're being unfair."

He looked at her. She was trying to help him, but she didn't really understand. How could she?

"I'll see you," he said, stepping out onto the porch and waving back at her.

It was colder, almost wintry. The moon was up, a thin crescent in the east, and the electric wires overhead hummed in the brittle air. He found his walking stick and headed up the boulevard. Now there was almost no traffic and his head buzzed, filled with the evening, his parents, the Bernsteins, the Book of Life. He thought about Buddy's limp. Buddy had been a fighter—not now, of course. Now he was a carpenter at that commune in New Mexico and they never heard from him except at Christmas when he would send a card. So what? What good was it? What did it mean? The words came into his mind like obscene random nonsense. Book of Life. Sign it. Promise.

Promise you'll never smoke weed. And no alcohol. Not even wine. Unbelievable!

At the railroad bridge he paused to watch a long freight train clanking through. The overpass jiggled and shook with the transmitted vibrations of iron banging on steel. He had played down there as a little kid, putting pennies on the tracks and scurrying away to wait as the train crushed them into wafers. Now the last flat cars were coming up, filled with giant spools of wire. Finally, the caboose went by and the sounds ebbed away in the night.

He walked along, hoping the Meeting would still be on when he got home so he could sneak up to his room and be asleep by the time his parents went to bed. He tried to get it all clear in his mind. He could give up smoking weed. No problem. But, there was something creepy about signing a book, a flat blue book with the Symbol printed in gold on the cover. Most if it was a kind of family tree with dates and names of people. In the center there were poems and at the end were the pledges.

As he came up the boulevard toward the school he could see the blue Pontiac parked in the same spot. Rice and the other kid were prying open a metal newspaper box with a crowbar. Rice gave a kick, toppling it and shattering the glass window. Newspapers fell out and spread across the sidewalk.

"Hey—cut it out!" Luke shouted. "What the hell are you doing?"

They looked across at him.

"What're you doing?" Luke yelled again, starting across toward them. They stood waiting. Luke walked slowly and gripped his stick. He didn't know what he was going to do, but suddenly he knew he was angry.

"Get out of here," he said.

They didn't answer.

"Go on, you freaks, get the hell out of here."

He stepped up on the sidewalk and walked over to them.

"Oh, yeah?" said the other kid. "Big man . . ."

Luke ignored him and looked Rice in the face.

"Go home, Rice," he said. "Get in your car and leave—now."

"Yeah, sure," Rice mumbled. "I dig you, man."

He started moving away. The other kid gave Luke a look that attempted disdain, but only the fear came through. The two of them got into the Pontiac. The engine started loud and the car shot away with a squeak of spinning, smoking rubber.

Luke watched the red lights disappear down the boulevard. His heart pounded and he felt warm. He stood over the newspaper box. They had succeeded in putting two large dents in it, and broken glass was all around, but the money compartment was secure.

He picked the thing up. It was a little unsteady, but he propped it against the front of the building. Then he took a final look around— and began walking home.

TAKE CARE OF EACH OTHER

I SHOULD GO HOME, BUT not just yet. How peaceful it is to sit here looking out at the quiet street in this Pennsylvania town where I've been a physician all these years.

Today is a holiday for the country—Labor Day—but several patients needed me, and the last of them left only minutes ago.

It's Monday—the first day of September, 1969.

The light filtering through the elm trees lends a soft, warm tone to the end of the afternoon, and a breeze nudges the hanging sign that stands on the patch of grass in front of my office:

Chaim Brodoff, M.D.
Family Practice

Thirty years ago today the Germans invaded Poland and bombed Cracow, the city where I was born.

September 1, 1939.

I was not there, for I had arrived in America one month before with my new medical diploma from the University of Bologna.

I never fail to note this day. Perhaps it's no more than a snapshot, an image faded with the passage of time, but it will always hold me. Thirty years in the new country are stripped away, and I am back in Europe.

Mostly I think about Joseph.

In the summer of 1933, Joseph Frankenthal and I traveled in a second-class railway carriage through the pine forests and wheat-fields of Poland and Czechoslovakia, and then, finally, after a few blurred glimpses of life in tidy Austrian mountain villages, we arrived in Italy to take up our new lives as medical students. It was to be a six-year program and we were eager to learn about the new country, to acquire a new language, and to adapt to a very different culture.

One day, after several months of settling in, we were wandering through the streets of Bologna on a sultry afternoon, exploring hopefully.

"I thought Italian women were insatiable," said Joseph, turning to watch the retreating figures of three girls to whom we had dared an enthusiastic *Buona sera*. Like startled birds they had fled with quick steps up the alley and disappeared around a corner.

"*Pazienza*," I reminded him. "We've barely arrived."

We turned into a larger street and mingled with a crowd of perspiring shoppers who shuffled slowly through the arcades. A hubbub of voices filled the humid atmosphere.

"'The women are insatiable.' I quote you, Don Juan Brodoff." Joseph was enjoying the tease. "Look at them all," he added.

"We just have to start talking to them," I said.

"With a dictionary maybe?"

"With our eyes."

Joseph grabbed my arm and held me back for a moment. "With our eyes? Do you remember when Mrs. Lipinski saw us watching her through the window?"

I looked at him and we burst into laughter. People stared at us and moved away. Children were racing about, and from somewhere above came the sounds of an operatic aria.

We came into a large open square. Along one side was an impromptu lingerie market. A vendor wearing a sleeveless undershirt and a fedora held up pink articles for inspection, but the women customers ignored his rapid-fire cajoling, and went on pawing through the garments and disparaging his prices.

"I don't think he has the knack," said Joseph.

We came to a large restaurant with tables out on the sidewalk.

"They look like fish," said Joseph, nudging me to look at the couples sitting there who watched with vague interest anything that passed. We sat down at an empty table.

"Let's try those cigars now."

Joseph handed me a black cigar. We ordered red wine and sat quietly sipping and blowing smoke rings.

"Goodbye, Cracow," I said after a while. "I feel free here. I love these old buildings—their tones. Cracow is drab and gray; Bologna is rich and brick-red."

Joseph sat looking out at the crowd.

"Do you like it?" I asked.

He flicked an inch of white ash from the cigar.

"I'm a little homesick," he said. "But, yes, I like it, too."

Now the light is fading into dusk. It's been almost an hour since my last patient left. I hear people walking along the sidewalk and cars starting up at the intersection. There is an airplane somewhere, probably one of those small planes from the flying club out at Ridgeview. Its engine surges, falters, and then revs up again.

And I'm remembering an article in The New York Times.

> ". . . A dense ground fog covered the Polish countryside today causing the Luftwaffe to miss many of its military targets. By mid-morning the weather had cleared and they came back again and again . . ."

Cracow fell on the sixth of September, 1939, and all of Poland on the twenty-seventh.

On a wet Friday evening in 1934 Joseph and I made our way along the cobblestoned alley leading to the Bologna synagogue. Beyond an arch and across a small court stood the yellow stucco building with a stained glass Mogen David mounted in the window over the doorway. We stood outside the arch for a moment.

"Maybe we shouldn't go in," I said, looking out into the drizzle as if there, in the gray air, I would find my excuse to leave.

"Anyone can go in," said Joseph. "And besides, I want to." He took hold of my arm and we stepped under the arch. Strange. In this, he was the decisive one. I would never have come alone, but now I was curious. It was uncharacteristic of Joseph to be so venturesome, but now I felt a little bolder as we walked across the crunching pebbles of the courtyard.

Heads turned as we tiptoed in and sat in the last row.

"Is it a *shul* or a church?" Joseph asked as we looked around at the people.

"Live and learn," I said. "You're the one who wanted to come." I was there grudgingly, irritated by Joseph's homesickness and clinging to old ways. All that inwardness and sorrow—I was happy to be rid of it. He had intimated several times that we ought to make a connection with the small Jewish community in Bologna, but I had left behind the tight scrutiny and strictures of Cracow and was determined to run free.

That morning I had been at the kitchen table trying to solve some chemistry equations. Joseph had finished his work and stood in the doorway sipping a glass of tea.

"I saw the *shul* the other day," he said. "It's not far."

"Wait, let me finish this." The symbols and numbers swam on the yellow page.

"Why don't we go there tonight?"

I threw him a noncommittal look, but he had a forlorn expression that I knew well. I nodded, and then got back to my work.

After the service there was an Oneg Shabbat with wine and food, and we stood about somewhat uncomfortably. Women, who had been sitting separately in an upstairs gallery, had come down and there was lots of talk and laughter. People smiled at us and someone gave us coffee and little pieces of cake. Finally, a very confident appearing man came up and introduced himself.

"I am Isaac Romano," he said, smiling and holding out his hand. "I am the president of the congregation." He was short and dressed in a dark suit.

"And you?"

We told him our story.

"Ah, Cracow—a lovely city. I import hides for the shoe industry and go abroad a good deal." He told us how his family had lived in Italy for generations and that Jews were allowed to live here in peace.

"I'm glad I don't live in Poland," he said. "The Poles could learn a lesson from Mussolini." What he was saying seemed right to me. I liked his directness.

"Things seem more progressive here," I said, looking around. "Men and women together. More freedom. More joy."

"We don't really know that," Joseph said to me in Polish. "We've only been here a few months."

"You know," Signor Romano continued. "I almost apologize to say it, but Poland really is one of the most backward countries I have visited."

"For Jews especially," I agreed.

Joseph struggled with his Italian. "Chaim means that we suffer exceptionally—more than the others."

A woman dressed in black came through the crowd followed by a dark haired girl.

"My wife and my daughter, Carla," said Signor Romano. We shook hands and after a few moments Signor Romano moved off to another group. Joseph and I stood smiling nervously at the two women. Signora Romano played with a heavy gold chain at her neck. Other people came over and joined us, and after brief greetings we seemed to blend into the larger group.

"You speak Italian very well," Carla said. She was seventeen and had the poise and candor of her father, but I only wanted to reach out and touch her smooth cheek. "Thank you," I said. "I love Italy. I would like to stay here forever."

She laughed

"How about you?" she asked Joseph. As she spoke, her chin jutted forward and I was very conscious of her lips moving.

Joseph put down his cup.

"I'm afraid I miss my family," he said, looking steadily at her.

"You must come to see us. Isn't that right, Mamma?"

Signora Romano nodded. "Of course," she said. "Anytime. Please come."

When we said good night I was startled to see Carla wink at us.

When I was eight years old my brother Dov was born and for a few weeks our home was full of light. Then, disappearing out of my life like an enigmatic dream, Father died suddenly. Dov, my mother, and I moved into two rooms in the old Ghetto: a bedroom, and a kitchen that served also as a sewing room. In one corner stood Mother's machine and the faceless mannequin whom I named Rivka and included in our family discussions.

Sometime later, Joseph Frankenthal, his parents, and two young sisters moved to Cracow from Russia and, in the manner of young schoolmates, he and I became friends.

We shared Passover Seders and often spent the evening of Shabbat with the Frankenthals, all special occasions in the marvelous comfort of their candle-lit dining room. Even now, after these many years, I can still see Mr. Frankenthal wrapped in his *tallit*, intoning prayers over the bread and wine, and can still recapture some of the happiness I felt being included in that enviable family.

It did not all go smoothly. Before Joseph's arrival I had been the undisputed student in my class, the teacher's prize pupil. Now Joseph often surpassed me and sometimes it became hard not to grow envious at his ease in learning. Secretly, I took some consolation in his general clumsiness, for he was stout and flat-footed and had a sallow, almost Mongol cast to his face.

When we were ten we once sneaked off and took an unsupervised excursion into the countryside. It began with a trolley ride to the outskirts of Cracow and then we meandered along the narrow roads, finally stopping at a certain farm.

"My grandfather had a farm like this in Russia," Joseph said. We were standing in the shade of some tall trees looking out into the bright glare of mid-day. Bees hummed in the air.

"He had a metal business, too," he boasted. "He even sold goods to the Czar"

"I don't believe you. Jews weren't allowed. You're always making things up."

He punched me in the shoulder and ran ahead into the wood. I chased him down the path and caught him, breathless, at the edge of the little stream that flowed there. We wrestled on the ground, tumbling on old leaves and then, satisfied and sweating, sat together on the mossy bank jabbing at the roots of trees with pointed sticks. Branches creaked overhead and the soft lowing of cows came to us from a nearby field.

"What will you do when you grow up?" I ventured after a while.

"I'm going to be a doctor," said Joseph. He told me about books his father had bought him. He knew all about atoms and chemistry and the symbols for the elements.

"Will you let me look at the books? Read them?"

"Sure. We're friends."

Joseph began to disappear from our Bologna apartment and gradually stopped reading for the courses we were taking. When I left in the morning he would still be under the blankets. During the day I might not see him at all and soon I stopped expecting him to return for supper in the evening. He would come in late, glance at me, and then go to sleep without a word.

So I began to spend more time with the other students, especially a group from Naples. They introduced me to Giuliana, a widow who accepted my virginity with grateful joy. I saw her for a while, but she was a dull woman and I soon lost interest in her.

One late afternoon I sat on a bench in the Piazza Maggiore, lulled by the peace of the twilight. The shadows lengthened on the cobblestones and pigeons fluttered and wheeled about me in great clumsy squadrons. It was a lonely moment and I was feeling that Joseph, my best friend, was lost to me. But that wasn't all. Something else, inexplicable, was also there. Guilt? Was I to blame?

Suddenly I caught sight of a couple, two figures walking arm in arm out of the cathedral of San Petronio. From his slouch and gait I recognized Joseph immediately, and the woman was very definitely Carla Romano. Joseph was oblivious, but Carla was already waving and pulling him along toward me.

"Hello," I said. "Been to Mass?"

"Very funny," said Joseph.

"How are you, Chaim? We never see you. Joseph, why don't you ever bring Chaim with you?"

Joseph was clearly peeved. I rose from my comfortable bench and Carla guided us to Pasquale, a small restaurant in the Viale Borromeo, where we drank coffee. Joseph was agitated. He couldn't endure to share Carla with anyone for even a brief moment.

"We'd better go now," said Joseph finally. "Doesn't your mother expect you soon?"

"I can stay out longer. Mother doesn't care. She trusts me."

Carla stretched back to take off her jacket. "Don't worry so much," she said. "Let's order some pizza and wine."

She leaned over, kissed Joseph on the cheek, and I tried to make my glances at her figure quick and unobtrusive.

That night Joseph and I talked.

"I'm going to marry her when we graduate," he said.

I was dumbstruck, but finally couldn't help myself.

"Do you think she can wait that long?" I asked. "She seems so . . . breathless."

"What do you mean? You like her, don't you?"

Was it possible that he really wanted my opinion?

"Oh, I just mean she seems, well . . . so mature. After all, you're talking about five years from now."

"She'll wait."

"You don't seem very happy," I noted.

He mumbled something, but I didn't make it out.

In the middle of the year Carla was sent off to a private school in Geneva. She had been slipping away at night to be with Joseph and when her parents discovered this they became frantic. At first Joseph was gloomy but then he suddenly developed great enthusiasm for his work, reading voraciously and studying for advanced courses. He wrote long letters to Carla and waited anxiously each day to see what the post would bring. Occasionally a blue envelope with exquisite handwriting would arrive from Switzerland and he would go off by himself for a few hours. The letters never cheered him. Finally a last blue envelope came. Joseph read the letter quickly, crumpled it up, and bolted from the room.

At midnight he returned to the apartment, opening the door very quietly.

"You're up," he said, surprised. "Sorry I ran off that way."

He was hanging up his coat and I couldn't see his face.

"What did the letter say?" I ventured.

He shut the closet door and sat down opposite me.

"It's all over," he said "She doesn't want to tie herself down. She's thought it all through. She's decided. So . . . that's it."

He looked tired. Defeated.

"Well," I started to say something reassuring. "She's . . ."

"Oh, it's probably all for the best. Crazy, eh? I mean, you were right. She's a tease."

"Look," I began. "In a way, it's fortunate for you. You might never have finished medicine."

Joseph didn't appear convinced. In the weeks that followed his mood was either wistful or dejected. I knew he kept the little pile of blue letters in the bottom drawer of his bureau. A few times I came back to the apartment to find him lying on his bed reading and re-reading them. He was a little embarrassed and made a clumsy joke about it, but gradually he was coming out of his depression. I forced him to come with me when I went out with the other students and in time he became a little more out-going. We began to live a pretty gay life. We even had a small lamp with a red light over a bookcase in the living room. If it was lighted it was a sign that one of us was entertaining a lady.

In May 1936, the Italian army finally defeated the ragged Ethiopians and the newspapers made much of the "glorious victory." All of us knew it was Mussolini's way of distracting the attention of the people from a steadily worsening economic situation.

One afternoon Joseph came out of the bedroom holding the packet of letters from Carla.

"I'm going to celebrate," he said. I looked up from my book.

"The end of the war?"

"No, I'm going to burn these."

He tore the letters, threw them into a metal waste-paper basket and set the shreds aflame.

"The end," he said, flapping his hand to wave away the smoke.

"What made you do it?"

"I think I've finally gotten over her," he said. He was looking down into the basket and poked at the sparks and smoking ashes.

Three years later on a bleak March day we stood at the back of the classroom, leaning against the wall with a few others who had been singled out by Professor Antonacci, only half-listening to his lecture on rheumatic fever. An unfortunate necessity, the Professor had said some weeks before with his tight little smile. Joseph and I, and the others, had listened quietly. No questions were asked. The Party had issued the decree. Jewish students would stand. We would be permitted to continue in the University, even to finish our studies. All that was required was that we stand in the back of the room. There was, Antonacci reminded us, a shortage of seats, and some people generally had to stand. This was merely a way of deciding who they would be.

Antonacci had been an unknown, a minor assistant in the department of pediatrics recognizable only by his nervous stammer, but he was a Fascist party member. Now, miraculously, he was Professor Antonacci. He had a small face with a prominence of canine teeth that made it difficult for him to close his mouth completely and his lips always had traces of moisture in the corners. His eyes were unusually large, giving him a startled look.

I paused in my note taking to pull my scarf up around my neck. There was no heat and all of the students wore coats. Antonacci himself wore a coat and gloves as he stood stiffly at the podium delivering his lecture. Joseph exchanged a glance with an American student, Weissman, standing alongside him.

"A real schmuck-hero," whispered Weissman, lifting an eyebrow toward the front of the room. "Someone for an aspiring doctor to imitate, eh?"

Joseph smiled and looked over at me.

"Weissman!" Antonacci cried out. "I saw that."

Eyes swept around. Weissman stared directly at Antonacci, the rabbit transfixed by the fox. A brittle silence filled the air for a long moment.

"You people are here on sufferance now," Antonacci said coldly, addressing those of us standing along the wall. "Don't forget it." He paused, surveyed the class, and went back to his lecture.

When it was over we stood about in small groups in the courtyard, talking and smoking. It was snowing, a muffled afternoon scene of white flakes drifting down from the gray sky. We made up one group, Joseph and Weissman, a few others and myself, all of us wanting to share in this latest episode of Antonacci's petty tyranny.

"The rat-faced bastard," one of the others blurted out.

"It's Germany," said Weissman. "Italians would never have thought of racial laws without pressure from the Nazis."

"We all know that," I said. "But Antonacci isn't unique. It's going to get worse."

We walked slowly down the street toward Piazza Galvani. The arcades were crowded with people. Housewives bundled up in scarves and dark overcoats pushed along with their shopping bags and children held by the hand. Men lounged about talking and gesturing, mostly about the new Pope, Cardinal Pacelli, wondering if he would stand up to the Germans. The Wehrmacht had completed its occupation of Czechoslovakia less than two weeks before and people were arguing about its meaning for Italy.

In the little bar we sat sipping wine in the same corner where Joseph and I had sat with Carla years before.

"What did I tell you last year?" Weissman was angry. "When Hitler came to Rome back then, what did I say?" Everyone nodded.

"Well, we'll be out of it soon," he went on. "In June we shall have our degrees."

"So what?" said Joseph, more than a hint of impatience in his voice. "You will be going home to New York. The rest of us . . ." He stopped.

Weissman lowered his eyes. "Isn't there a chance of your going to some British place? Are you sure you've exhausted that?" he asked, looking around at the rest of us.

All that spring we debated what to do. I insisted we make some plans about our future, but Joseph seemed strangely apathetic. He felt he would return to Cracow, to his family.

"I'll never go back," I said.

He ignored me.

I shoved a copy of *La Vita Italiana*, the fascist newspaper, at him.

"Look at this," I said. "Look at their lies. Did you know that Roosevelt is a Jew? Rosenfeld?"

He gave me a pained look.

"Ciano is in Berlin negotiating with von Ribbentrop," I told him. "Things will get steadily worse for us. We have to make up our minds."

In April Joseph agreed to go with me to the British Consul in Florence to request visas for India. A crowded bus took us over the pass and down into the flowering valley of the Arno. The city sprawled before us in an extravagant array of red tiled roofs and wondrous domes. In the consulate office we waited for hours in a room filled with other petitioners. We finally had our turn in the little room, standing before the deputy consul. I looked down at our passports flattened on the desk in front of him, each stamped with the word *Hebrew*.

"I'm sorry," he said. "We cannot . . ."

"We are willing to go anywhere in India. We will work for next to nothing."

"I know," he said. "And I regret this, but I can do nothing." He swept up the passports and handed them back to us.

Joseph returned to Bologna, but I decided to try the British embassy in Rome. I was back in two days.

"Sorry," I explained quietly. "Another failure."

A few weeks went by. We were sitting in the living room reading when someone banged on our door. It was Weissman. He had raced up the stairs and staggered into the room as if he had run three miles. He could hardly talk.

"Come on. I think I've got you visas to America," he sputtered out the details. "They may take you because you'll have medical degrees."

We looked at him astonished.

"But they have a quota on Poles," said Joseph.

"No, they can get around it because you're not current residents of Poland. You've been living in Italy for six years."

It was a miracle! We danced around the room, holding each other and kissing Weissman's cheeks.

"I'll just be in Cracow during the summer," Joseph said. "Then I can meet you later in New York."

He was full of doubts. His father wanted him to return home in June.

"I don't think you should delay," I cautioned.

He held a letter in his hand, the crowded lines of black ink telling him that his mother was ill.

"I know, I know," he said. "He says to come back at least for the summer to see if I can get some sort of position."

"Position! As what—a street cleaner? Joseph, your father doesn't understand. Don't you realize that? Poland will be next."

"Even if I can't get work as a physician, he says he wants me to help him in the mill."

"The mill! There won't be any mill. Look, go to your parents. See them for a few days. Wish them well. Then say goodbye. We have to go to America."

"We'll see," he murmured.

"I'm telling you. If you want to go to America, it had better be soon."

"I'm not sure. It is such a long way. And we can't speak the language. Do you realize how hard that will be?"

"Joseph, we learned to speak Italian. We'll learn to speak English."

"It's true. Oh, I don't know. If the Germans invade and there is war..."

"If there is war, Joseph, we'll all be running—you, me, everyone. Being a rabbit doesn't help the other rabbits who are hunted."

"I need more time to think."

"Think," I said, heading for the door. "I'll see you later."

I felt his worried eyes following me, but I didn't want to sit in that room any longer, endlessly reiterating the dilemma, and I was tired of trying to drag him along.

It was dark on the stairs, and the sun and clatter of the street stunned and bedazzled me when I stepped outside. As I strolled along past the flower stands and fish carts I realized that, with or without Joseph, I would be leaving Italy very soon. We had lived here six years. Something, some scent (What was it?) drew my mind back to the day we had left Poland so long ago. Truly, it had been another era.

The Cracow station had been crowded on our day of departure in 1933. The westbound train had arrived from Lvov and in the smoky light of early morning people began filing on board. At one corner of the waiting room some peasants had set out flowers for sale and the fresh scent of lilac diffused into the sour air. Our families had gathered to say goodbye. We stood there in a sad little group, aloof from other travelers, and a bit awkward. Joseph's young sisters stood quietly, holding hands with their mother, frightened by the noise and the sight of so many people.

My brother, Dov, stood next to me. He looked like a little man in the tightly fitting jacket with its velvet collar that my mother had made.

"What is it like in Italy?" he asked.

"I don't know," I replied. Fear and uncertainty moved across his face like wind on a lake. I could see myself in his features, my apprehension mirrored and cast aback at me. I embraced him.

"Shall I sent you a picture card when I get there?"

"Oh, yes," he begged.

I was impatient. Joseph was hugging his mother. She cried, and then kissed his pale face. He looked to me.

"Come on," I said, pulling his sleeve. "We'd better go." I kissed my mother who looked frail and thin in her dark brown dress.

"Be careful," she said. She grasped me by the shoulders and as I bent to kiss her I glimpsed the tiny cup-like earrings swinging gently in quick little arcs from the soft downy lobes. A hint of camphor rose from the wool of her coat.

Joseph's father held us each by a hand, his remote, sunken little eyes flaring and magnified by thick rimless lenses. He bent to kiss Joseph.

"Papa, write frequently," said Joseph.

I looked down at the platform.

"Goodbye, Chaim," said Mr. Frankenthal. I felt his wiry beard against my cheek as he leaned forward to hug me. "Take care of each other."

We broke away and pushed toward the train.

The compartments were filled and we climbed into a second-class carriage just as the train began to move. We waved back at the little group on the platform, the train went around a slight curve, and quickly there was only the cement wall alongside the track to be seen.

The car was crowded with peasants traveling to small villages outside the city. The train picked up speed.

"Seats down at the end," said Joseph, gesturing with his suitcase. We made our way through the car, stepping carefully. A short droll-looking man with a dirty hat sat next to the aisle, arms folded, a smirk on his face. His wife sat alongside, a heavy woman with a child at her breast. He put his leg out, blocking our way.

"Where are you going, Jew?"

"Excuse me. We would like to get by."

"Stop that," the woman ordered gruffly, pulling him quickly toward her. The man pulled in his leg and spat on the floor. There was a burst of choked laughter, then wet coughing from the seats nearby.

We sat down at the end of the car. Numb. Silent.

Now we were passing through the outskirts of the city. Smoke drifted up from chimneys and I could see a few people walking along on their way to work or to market. To the south were the tall mountains of Carpathia, green forest covering their steep sides.

We were on our way.

Mr. Frankenthal's words lingered: *Take care of each other.*

Of course, but wasn't that something you said to children? It seemed old-fashioned to me. We were going to become doctors. We could certainly take care of ourselves if we were going to take care of other people.

I looked across at Joseph. His eyes were closed, and after a few moments so were mine.

My watch reads a quarter to six. I gather my things, drink a glass of water, and head out to my car. I know I'll be home in twenty minutes, but it's as if I'm sleepwalking. This is Pennsylvania, but I'm not quite here. What I see is myself meeting Carla that wonderful afternoon in late May. I see her walking toward me across the little park.

"Chaim!"

We stood uncomfortably for a moment. I stammered a few bits of nonsense, and she almost managed to put me at ease with her marvelous poise, but I was already embarrassed and close to trembling with excitement. We sat down on a bench and I caught a whiff of her perfume. She seemed older. And still warm and alluring.

"You're looking well," she smiled.

We laughed a little.

"Will you have some coffee with me?" I asked.

She agreed, and we went into a dim little bar. Carla had lived in Geneva for four years and had worked for a friend of her father's in an import-export business. Now she had returned to Italy only to find that her father never left his bedroom and talked of nothing but suicide. Her mother suffered from daily attacks of panic. Over everything hung the uncertainty and fear that defined the mood of the year. I told her of my plan to go to America after I took my degree.

"And Joseph? What will he do?" she asked. I was surprised at the question. Did she still have a feeling for him?

"I'm trying to convince him to do the same. It's difficult. His family is still there . . ."

"And your family?"

"My mother and brother have left Cracow. They got visas for England and they are in London. I have no reason to return to Poland."

She picked up some crumbs of bread from the tablecloth with a moistened finger and flicked them into her mouth.

"And so Joseph . . ."

". . . is torn. He can't make up his mind."

"Poor man." She leaned against the wall of the little booth, the candlelight flickering on her cheek.

"And you, and your parents?"

"I don't know," she said "At times Father talks about going away, perhaps to Ethiopia. Others are going there. But he doesn't seem to be able to make a decision. Mother is no help. Everything falls on me. If they decide, I'm the one who'll have to move them. They're like helpless children."

Her lips moved slowly. My hand rested on the table and suddenly she reached out and covered it with her own. Her eyes were brimming with tears. I drew her to me and held her against my chest.

"Chaim," she murmured. "I'm sorry."

Her hair brushed my lips and I could feel the softness of her body.

"I should go," she said.

"Will you come to the apartment?"

She looked at me steadily, but said nothing.

"No one is there," I said.

"Joseph . . ."

I shook my head. "He's got something else tonight."

She turned away.

"Carla . . . I want to be with you."

She faced me again. "Yes," she said, nodding quickly. "I'll come."

We left the bar and walked along the little alley. It was dark now.

When I awoke, Carla was lying next to me, sound asleep with her arms thrown back under her hair. The clock showed ten-fifteen and I nudged her side gently.

"We'd better go. I don't know when he'll be back."

A small lamp in the corner cast shadows over the rumpled bedclothes Carla curled up facing me. I leaned over and kissed her again.

"Chaim, you don't have to. I mean . . . we're both . . ."

"Ssssh . . don't talk; don't say anything."

We dressed hurriedly.

"When will I see you again?" I asked. She had her back to me, brushing her hair and looking at my reflection in the mirror.

"I can meet you in the park," she said.

A moment later we heard steps in the hall and a key in the door. Stupidly, I hadn't turned on the red light, but the futile thought came too late. I held up my hand and put a finger to my lips. Joseph was already in the front room.

"Chaim! Chaim, I've decided. Chaim? Are you here?"

Carla's hand went up to her mouth as she spun around.

"Chaim . . ."

Joseph stood there, not moving, looking at us as his eyes took in the room and the bed.

"Joseph . . ."

He stared, moving his head in disbelief, then suddenly turned and ran out of the apartment.

We spoke little after that time.

In July, Joseph returned to Poland.

Thanks

To my children and grandchildren, to my friends and patients, and to many people I have met in my work and in my travels. I've learned from all, and this quirky tapestry owes much to them.

And, always, to Sue . . . for everything.

About the Author

William M. Gould, a creature of habit with a short attention span, is still to be found in Northern California practicing medicine, playing jazz, and messing around with words.

Printed in the United States
By Bookmasters